# LOOKING FOR MARIANNE

OCT 0 0 2021
SKANEATELES LIBRARY ASSOC
49 E. Genesee
Skaneateles, NY 13152

# LOOKING FOR MARIANNE

*a novel*

**Ron Iannone**

Destination Press
Morgantown, West Virginia

*Looking for Marianne*
© 2021 Ron Iannone

ISBN: 978-0-9982020-6-8

This title is also available as an audiobook.

This is a work of fiction. All names, characters, places, and incidents, are products of the author's imagination, or are used fictitiously. Any resemblance to actual events or persons, living or dead, is entirely coincidental.

Cover photograph: Justin Iannone

## Also by Ron Iannone

*Alternatives to the Coming Death of Schooling*

*"School Ain't No Way..." Appalachian Consciousness*

*Consequences: Short Stories, Poems, Commentaries*

*A Boston Homecoming*

*A Not So Normal Family*

*An Ethnic Connection and Goals Beyond: Reflections of an Italian American Poet, Second Edition*

*Voices on the Edge: Plays & Screenplays, 1980–2018*

*To those who are suffering with mental illness, especially depression. Yes, treatment can be found in pills, but what's best in penetrating the dark clouds hovering above is the love of a friend or the touch of a significant other.*

*Our lives are like the sea,
Its surface distorts
Its innermost depths,
And so with us
Our lives become a lie
And our souls hide
In the shadows
Of our tomorrows.*

—Peter Franklin

**Looking for Marianne**

December 21, 2019

Dear Freddy,
I know you are getting my messages. Please, please call or write me!!

Paul

**Looking for Marianne**

January 1, 2020

Dear Freddy,
I don't know why you're not calling or writing. I know the trial has been over for at least two months. I need to talk to you. I got ideas for the appeal.

Best,<br>Paul

**Looking for Marianne**

January 5, 2020

Dear Freddy,
I saw an article about me in the paper. Did you see it? They say without a doubt I killed Marianne.

Paul

January 20, 2020

Dear Freddy,
I need to go back over the case now. I think so many things were left out about me. Are you ever going to write or call me?

Paul

February 1, 2020

Dear Freddy,
I need to explain everything. You really didn't have all the facts for the trial. I'm going to tell you the truth the best I can. So this letter may be long.

At times, I'll be confused, but I'll try to get everything out. I want to get out of here. Yesterday some guy pushed me and wanted to start a fight. A prison guard saw it and got him away from me. Anyway, I just hate this place. The noise is killing me. At least I have some free time to write to you and my children. They let me keep a computer in my cell. This place is a hell on earth. It's a violent and dirty place with crappy food. Gray, tan, cream, or sick green walls all the time.

I'm forty-six years old, and I can't believe I'm in here for twenty years with perhaps parole fifteen years from now. The police were awful. Thank God for you. I know you didn't have much time to prepare for the trial. You did the best you could.

I guess it comes down to this. I don't know if I killed Marianne. You need to know more about me, more than I told you before the trial. I want to convince you to move on my appeal faster. I'm not sure if you really believe I'm not guilty.

Here's what I plan to do. I hope in this letter to tell you the full story. Clarity and truth will be my guide throughout. At times, I know I will ramble, as my students will say I did in class. But I'll try, as I said, to do my best to remember all my interactions with significant people in my story. Some of this story you have heard before as you prepared for the trial, while some other parts will be new. And I apologize for not telling or remembering at the time all of it.

Another thing I don't know—where I'll be going with my writing to you. Even though I'm supposed to be a writer, I'm also lazy. Writing is hard work. Before I write to you it will probably take me five or six drafts before I'm clear. I want to be as honest as I could, even though sometimes you'll see it sounds like shit. But I'll try my best. I've been here in Auburn Correctional Facility for nearly sixty days. I met a guy in the yard the other day who has been here for over twenty years. He's a former math teacher who had an affair with one of his students and then chopped her up and buried her. Nice guy, huh. And you know what? He seems very quiet to me. He seems to have accepted his fate. He said he read about my case in the newspapers. He wants to know more but I won't tell him. I want it to all come out in my appeal.

You see, Freddy, I lie a lot and so I got to get through all my lies to get to the truth. There's so much I need to tell you. I don't know if I killed her, but I don't like what the newspapers are saying. Her leg just slipped out of my hand. The jury never got the full truth.

I know you said after I was convicted that you were going to work on the appeal. However, I was screwed in the trial. Can you tell me where you are on the appeal? I know you're busy but it would be great to see you. I don't want to end up like the math teacher. He said he couldn't believe a Harvard graduate like me was in prison. I can't either. There're some other things I need to tell you about myself.

First, they try to keep us busy in here. There are counts in prison. They start at the same times each day: 5 a.m., 11:30 a.m., 4 p.m., 9 p.m., and midnight. You always hear, "Five minutes till count time, people," blaring over the PA system in the same dull, unsympathetic voice that repeats these words multiple times a day, every day. "Be on your bunks and be visible for the 11:30 count or you will get a ticket." Such bullshit!!!

I worry that one of these hard guys who looks rough and tough is going to beat me up. I try hanging out with the guy who chopped up his student. For some reason they seem to be afraid of him. At least I feel I fit in with him. Hopefully they will leave me alone. They also hate child abusers. There's a priest in here that abused I heard over twenty children. He's been beaten up so many times that his face looks like a dart board.

## Looking for Marianne

I still don't understand why you couldn't get bail while you appealed. Anyway, I have to begin with some of my personal history.

My father, James, was an owner of a grocery chain. I hardly saw him because of his work, drink, and whoring around. My mother, Beth, was an elementary school teacher and hated being a parent. Deep down, I think both my parents really hated kids, even though my mother worked with them all day. She told me once she was too nervous for kids. That's why they decided to send me off to a boarding school outside of Syracuse when I was a teenager. The school was called Riverdale. We were living nearby in a middle-class suburb called Manlius. I went to the Manlius High School for the first two years of high school.

After I started Riverdale in my junior year, my parents decided to buy a larger home on the lake in Skaneateles, New York. Marianne was also from there. We never really knew each other because while I was in Riverdale she was attending a private school in Syracuse called Peddle Hill. We met while we both attended University of Rochester. There's where we fell in love with each other. Now, I don't think it was love, it was about sex.

Riverdale was a military school. My parents thought that was good, especially my mother. Her nerves couldn't handle the expected discipline that came along with raising a teenager.

Freddy, I know the appeal will take a long time, but in the new trial I want everything to come out, I mean

I want people to know how complicated I am. In short, my friend, I want the truth about me to come out.

There is something else I need to tell you about what happened at Riverdale. I know it was brought up briefly, but you got the judge to dismiss it because it was not relevant to the present proceedings. I think I didn't tell the full truth about what happened at Riverdale.

Freddy, I was involved in witnessing a classmate of mine murdered. There were three classmates who did it. I watched and helped bury the body. But that's all.

Since that time, the memory of that night causes me to break out in cold sweats and even black out if I get so panicked about it. I will explain the whole black-out thing later on.

– – –

A few years ago, I went back to Riverdale with Marianne for our 25th reunion. I also was hoping with everyone but Billy being there, we could finally deal with what happened that night.

For me, when I think about that night, it's very cloudy and everything is framed in white. As Aaron kept screaming, "I'm fucking drunk, I'm fu—" Billy moved quickly in front of him, shouldered the rifle, and shot him in the forehead. Then Billy handed the rifle to Henry who shot him in the chest. Then he handed the rifle to Jim who shot him in the crotch. Quickly, Billy grabbed the rifle from Jim and began laughing, "We are free now, free! Thank you, God."

Still laughing crazily. Pure and simple, he was completely insane as he ran deep into the woods. I would never see him again.

For a few seconds, I thought I saw for a moment exhilaration on all their faces. Almost glee. Perhaps Billy was right they felt for a moment or two free ... We buried Aaron under a good-sized aluminum container that was nearby. It was a corroded old thing, back in the bushes, maybe left from when they tore down the old heating plant. Aaron's blood was splattered all over us.

– – –

Last year Jim had emailed me that Billy was dead; he said it was suicide. His body was discovered a couple months before at the bottom of Fall Creek Falls near Cornell. There is a gorge nearby made up of rock, water, and trees. You can get to the gorge from Linn Street in downtown Ithaca. We had all been there several times to drink beer and vodka, and picnic with freshman girls from Cornell. The police said there was evidence on the way down the 400-foot drop that Billy tried grasping for grass and small trees.

– – –

When we arrived at the Riverdale campus for the reunion, I became very nervous. We found the desk to register underneath an open-sided tent. And while we were registering, I saw Jim and Henry approaching. Jim and Henry looked about the same as they did in school. Jim was bulkier, with thinning sandy hair, and Henry looked great; the years of jogging and biking seemed to have paid off. If Billy had been there, he probably would be a little fatter. He had bright red hair, a moon face, with huge blue eyes. Everything about him was really pudgy, even his fingers. Soon we are all shaking hands and hugging. Both were impressed with Marianne's beauty, even though her depression made her look worn out and fatigued. Her grayish hair mixed with chestnut curls, a milky complexion, and soulful brown eyes made her stand out in the midst of other women in their forties.

On the way to the table assigned to our class, I found out that Jim was working in Syracuse at U.S. Steel as vice president of accounting. He was divorced, had two children who were doing well in Seattle, and he also mentioned he had a girlfriend. Sometimes he said he volunteered at Riverdale to help raise funds. Henry was also divorced, with no children, and ran his father's publishing business called Lakeside Publishing, which specialized in murder mysteries. It was located in Glenn Falls, New York.

While we now sat at our assigned table, Jim and Henry flirted with Marianne. She loved it.

A good part of the afternoon, we drank beer, and ate clams and barbecue chicken. We tried to listen to former alumni talk about how Riverdale changed their lives, but our minds were on something else.

Afterwards, Jim took us around campus, which looked old and worn-out. During the tour, Jim made Henry and me pledge $50,000 each for the building campaign. Just as it was turning dark, we ended up at the Washington Tavern where we used to go after school for shakes, hamburgers, hot dogs, and great fries. The chain restaurant *Steak 'N Shake* is no better than the tavern.

Before we sat down at a table in the rear, Marianne said she was going back to the hotel. She was tired, she said. And she looked it, with large black circles now appearing under her eyes.

After she left we placed our order for beer and fries. Alcohol was served on reunion weekends. And for a long moment no one said anything. Finally, Jim asked quietly, "Do any of you ever think of Aaron?"

I said, "Almost every day. Should we now talk about it after all these years? I mean, we never did after that day. I think we pretended it never happened. The police told his parents that he ran away to Europe like a lot of rich kids did then. After that I think we all buried it in our memories"

"I also got some information about Aaron's parents," Jim said.

"Good," I said.

"His parents just donated two million dollars to Riverdale to name the new theatre in Aaron's name."

"Hell, he never showed any interest in theatre," I said. "All he wanted to do was to sneak out and get drunk."

"You remember I volunteer here in the development department," Jim said, "and the director, a real talker, convinced the parents he did love theatre. Even though we all know that's bullshit like you said, Paul."

"Hey, remember," Henry said, "we used to write his love letters to his pimple-faced girlfriend, Lola. Aaron just didn't have the vocabulary or the understanding of adjectives and adverbs. Mister Darling worked his ass off trying to get him to understand when to use them."

"I know," I said.

"Yeah," Henry now said. "Remember he would get nervous when speaking in class and he would end up saying, 'He neither was supposed to do it.' These days maybe a school speech therapist would help with something like that."

For the next few hours we drank a lot of beer as we caught up with our lives until Jim brought up Aaron again.

"We got to do something about Aaron," he said.

"I agree," I said as Henry nodded in agreement. "I think about Aaron with his pudgy angelic face that had freckles running across his nose. I wonder why his body was never found after all these years? And why the hell did Billy bring an M16 that night?"

"To shoot birds," Jim said.

"Please," Henry said, "that's crazy. It was in the middle of the night."

"I know," Jim said, "Mr. Darling also told us earlier in class that day how to free ourselves from the material world so the divine could enter our souls. That's why we really went out that night."

"I remember," I said, "also how we fasted all day but ate junk food in the evening. Then we drank gin and vodka. Remember Mr. Darling said St. Theresa of Ávila and St. John of the Cross fasted all the time. I doubt they ate junk food and drank gin and vodka. Anyway, they did the fasting so the divine could live in them. Darling said Greeks would have these celebrations where they fasted too, and through meditation and prayer they moved into the spiritual realm and lost the material world."

"Hell," Jim continues, "remember also Darling talked about that Russian writer. What was his name, Oupsen? Oh I know now—it was Ouspensky."

"Darling was really into some weird stuff, but regardless he was a great teacher," Henry said.

"I still can't believe after all these years they never found him," Jim said.

"Right," Henry agreed. "I thought we'd get off on manslaughter charges if they caught us. Paul, you didn't do anything except help us bury him. I still don't understand why you didn't."

Suddenly I got up. "Let's see if we can find him. That container, if it's still there, is somewhere directly in back of the tavern here."

Being quite dark, we used our iPhones as flashlights and after a few minutes we found the old corroded aluminum container. We quickly moved it and begin to dig underneath until Henry started to yell, "Shit, I found his skull." Shaking uncontrollably, he held it up and we shone our phones on it as if it were a treasure.

Jim screamed, "Put it back!"

So we began burying the skull with leaves and dirt. All three of us lifted and replaced the container back onto Aaron's skull.

— — —

As we walked back to the tavern, I asked, "Should we go to the police?"

"No," Henry said. "Let it be or we'll all be ruined."

"I agree," Jim said.

"I'll kill myself before I go to jail," Henry added.

"I don't know if I can live with the guilt," I said.

"Fuck the guilt—Paul, you really didn't do anything" Jim said. I just want to live.

Little did I know then, Freddy, that I would be in jail for murder. Not for Aaron, but for Marianne.

Afterwards, Jim drove me back to the hotel, and just before I opened the car door to leave, he leaned over and touched my arm. "Forget it, Paul. If you need to talk, call, okay?"

"Okay," I said remorsefully. I closed the door and walked toward the entrance of the hotel. Still in my mind I could see the blood dripping from Aaron's lips.

A few years ago Marianne and I were in Bulgaria on a river cruise. Her parents paid for it because they thought it would help with our marriage and Marianne's depression. Anyway, while there I thought

I saw Aaron in the distance from an outside café we were eating at. He looked fit and happy. He was about the same age as when he died. So I got up and walked in his direction and saw a small, burned hole in the middle of his forehead. He smiled at me, and as I got closer, he vanished.

– – –

You see, Freddy, everything seemed to be changing over the last few years between Marianne and me. Thank God I had Abby and my teaching at Cayuga to help me forget that night at Riverdale. Also, drinking wine helps. You know over the years I've had a few affairs with other students, but nothing real serious until I met Abby.

It was about two years ago, she was enrolled in two of my classes. I noticed at first she had a pretty face except for a scar on her right cheek. I would find out later she was a veteran of three tours in Afghanistan. She had other scars too, which you could only see when her clothes were off.

I noticed also in her student file that she had received a Bronze Star medal. She would never talk about it. But I looked up Bronze Star on my cell phone and discovered that the medal was awarded to individuals who distinguished themselves in a combat theater by heroism or meritorious survival. I was impressed, and was always impressed by what service veterans have done for us. After I got to know her, I learned she still suffered with pain from her wounds. The pain she said goes away for a while with pills. There was something in her eyes. Either there's someone home or there isn't. Either you want to knock on that door or you don't. Her eyes were green, and they were warm and liquid with some kind of dreamy satisfaction. We often met at the fitness center and then would go to her place and make love.

During this time as I was falling in love with Abby, Marianne's depression began to sink lower. She talked to me about starting a business making necklaces and bracelets with colorful beads. In the early years of our marriage, I remembered she would craft different pieces and even make figurines like animals and children figures. If she did start the business, I knew she was bright enough for the business end. She was always good with numbers. I thought nothing would come of this idea though because of her deepening depression. In the past, she had ideas of starting a shoe store, wine and cheese bookstore, children's clothing store, and on and on, but it went nowhere.

– – –

One time during our early years of marriage she tried committing suicide by throwing herself down the stairs from the second floor. Except for a small bruise on her head, she was okay. Before this, I found her in our bathroom late at night with razor blades trying to cut her wrists. We told the ER people later she was cutting vegetables and the knife slipped. The doctors knew we were lying, but they gave us a pass. Jesus, who the hell is cutting vegetables at two in the morning?

– – –

Rose, her mother, told me she was worried about her and her depression. She said Marianne would call her every time she was running outside on paths near the lake and if no one was around, she would scream and cry while running. She told me she would scream over and over, "I can't take this! Make it stop! The demons, Mom, won't stop! God, please turn it off!" She would keep screaming these things until she got hoarse and her voice vanished completely.

Then according to Rose, Marianne would slow down and fast walk. All the while, talking to Rose about her worries, especially not having enough money to pay bills. So she told Rose she wanted to start a bead company now and would Rose give her money to begin the company. Of course, Rose told her yes. She would do anything to help Marianne find some peace in her life. Little did Marianne know how bad our financial problems were.

Marianne's therapist was also costing us about a thousand a month. We had too much money going out and not enough coming in. However, she said the therapist was helping, but the therapist was now pissed off at her, because the therapist felt Marianne was not working hard enough to get out of her depression, which was getting more serious.

The other day Marianne told me she had problems with the in-between world ... when nothing is happening ... she felt brain dead.

However, when she was rushing around delivering some of the finished bead artwork and driving Jake to his appointments, she felt okay. Our son, Jake, had a slight case of autism, and had to be taken to his cognitive specialist every morning at 7:30, whereas our daughter, Sara, had to be at middle school at 8:05. Then, if there was a PTA meeting in the morning, she would attend. She liked to keep herself busy, she said because her mind felt like it was exploding sometimes. The schedule and running around helped her. But I couldn't stand it, and I think that was another reason I fell in love with Abby. The distance between Marianne and me was getting wide while Abby and I were almost becoming one.

– – –

One night I didn't want to go home after teaching an evening class. Marianne's bitching and her depression were getting to be too much. I should go home, I thought, and talk to her about wanting a divorce and loving Abby. But not tonight. I just wanted to forget her and relax a little. So I decided to stop and get a drink at the Sherwood Inn, which was down the street from where we lived in Skaneateles. As I sat down on the far end of the bar, I saw at the other end a stately looking woman. She was wearing a white turtleneck sweater, her blonde hair fell perfectly from her shoulders. She was beautiful.

Now I recognized her, it was Sandra Brown, the famous TV personality who interviewed major stars and news-makers. She looked over at me for a second, then turned back to the bartender she was talking to. And soon, she looked over again. She stood up, smiled at me, paid the bartender, and left. Another opportunity I missed out on, I thought. There have been so many opportunities with women I missed out on because I was too shy to make the first move. I remembered the love-starved nun who I had in class and who wrote these weekly pornographic letters to me about how much she loved me and would do anything to satisfy me. Marianne and I were Catholic but we never really went to church. We were married in the Catholic church and our kids were baptized. But that's it. Once all the abuse stuff came out, priests abusing little children, we completely stopped going. *Anyway, I couldn't see myself making love to a nun.* As I was drinking my second glass of wine, I thought about this morning's argument. In so many words, I told Marianne I didn't know where I belonged. I hated having so many rich people all around us. When we were with them the talk was always about what new car they bought or how they were putting in a new pool with fountains and walls and decorating their exotic flower gardens. Marianne said I should accept it. That's life. Bullshit, I said. I wanted to be with people who talked about plays, music, paintings.

I do understand why young people moved away from Skaneateles. They wanted excitement in their lives. Sometimes I thought that after I leave Marianne, perhaps Abby and I can move to New York City like she wanted, where the beautiful and smart people are. I needed to find a way to get the divorce from Marianne and live with Abby for the rest of my life. I needed to talk to people who could expand my mind. People around Skaneateles and at the college are not interested in talking about truth and the purpose of life. I wanted friends who would call me daily and really care about how I was doing. I wanted friends who would drop whatever they are doing so they can be with me.

– – –

Freddy, finally I told Marianne about our possible bankruptcy in the future. We had almost run out of my inheritance of one million dollars from my grandparents.

"How could that be?" she asked.

"I invested in a small tech company that was working on a promising artificial intelligence application, and it flopped. Sorry."

"What are we going to do?"

"I'm going to try to borrow on my retirement funds from the college and work more."

"What about food and stuff like that?" she asked, worried.

"Don't worry, I still have a little money left. We'll get by," I said.

"Why didn't you tell me sooner?"

"I just didn't want to worry you. I really thought the company, which was called Full Potential, was a sure thing. However, when I stopped getting calls from the CEO Steve Klein, I knew something was wrong."

"I can ask my parents," she said.

"I'm sorry, your parents do so much for us already," I said. "Too bad my father had blown it all away on women and drink."

– – –

One afternoon, Marianne asked me if I was going to be at Sara's gymnastics meet that evening.

"I'm working on a couple of articles with a colleague so I can get promoted next year," I lied. The last night with Abby, I thought she'd brought me to a world I've never been. Her touch made my whole body vibrate. I never ever felt like that.

"Paul, are you having an affair with someone?" she asked bluntly. "You're gone so many nights. I know Sara really wants you there."

"I know but I'm almost finished. And no, I'm not having an affair. We got to get more money, and publications will help me get promoted and get a raise."

"I know. Well, next time," she said, "try to make it for Sara's sake. She loves you so much."

– – –

Soon I'd get to deal with the whole divorce issue between Marianne and me. I'm finding it very difficult to live with my mind always on Abby. Her love for me is an almost obsessive love, reminds me a little of Shirley Feinstein who I dated off and on while I was at Riverdale and Harvard. In fact, she still emails me constantly about how much she loves me and wants to take care of me. In her last email to me, she said that her husband had Alzheimer's, and she was the major caretaker, Freddy. And I know that you don't know this. After Marianne was only missing a day, I flew out and met Shirley in New York City at her sister's place. See, Freddy, I never had anyone who loved me so passionately. At least four or five times a year she would come to visit me wherever I was. This time, however, I needed to see her. I never had a woman who swallowed me up totally in love and sex, not even with Abby. I also knew this thing, with Marianne gone, it was going to get really bad. And I needed to forget the whole missing thing for at least a few hours. Shirley knew how to make me feel wanted and powerful. But just like what happens when you get a buzz from alcohol, the next day you're sick and depressed.

– – –

The night before meeting Shirley, I was at Abby's when suddenly we heard a loud banging coming from a downstairs door. Abby lived in a two-story condo. We both quickly dressed. The banging continued.

**Looking for Marianne**

Abby ran down the stairs as I stood above her on the second-floor landing, looking down. She opened the door and I could see Marianne with a bright red face, crying. "Is Paul here?" she sobbed and looked up at me.

"Yes, he is," Abby answered.

"I see you up there, asshole. How could you, how could you?" she screamed looking up at me. She turned and angrily left.

Abby looked up at me and was crying. "What are you going to do?"

"I got to tell her about us." I said as I now brushed by her, running into the dark night.

— — —

Freddy, I drove all over Skaneateles looking for Marianne that night. When I got home, nobody was there. The kids were gone and Marianne was gone. So I called Marianne's parents, Bill and Rose Allen. They were both retired now and always willing to watch the kids if we were going out or going away for a weekend. Rose recently retired from teaching at the same Skaneateles elementary school for thirty-five years. Bill just recently retired from Syracuse University where he taught math and computer classes. He went in every so often and also had royalties coming in from a computer component he invented that every computer made needs. In short, they were wealthy. I thought of them as good and kind grandparents to the kids.

Rose answered and said, "Marianne came over and just dropped the kids off. She needed to get away for a while, she said, because she said you two had an argument." Thank God, Marianne didn't tell her about finding me at Abby's.

I asked, "Did she say exactly where she was going?"

"No," Rose said. "She just said she had to get away."

"Call me if she calls or comes back. I'll do the same."

– – –

At the time Marianne went missing my love for Abby was strengthening and becoming a lifelong love. Sometimes in class I could hardly keep my eyes off her. Her body was slender and somewhat concave, where the wounds were. I learned from her, as she began to open up a little, that an IED almost destroyed her not only physically but mentally. As I said earlier, Freddy, she never talked about what really happened in her tours in Afghanistan and with an IED. But she did talk to me about wanting to finish her degree. She was using the GI money to pay for her tuition. After her degree, she wanted to go to New York or Paris to work in the art world. Her dream was to be rich and famous and now she wanted me to come along. I told you before I had Abby in class I met her at the local fitness center. She was very interested in her health and keeping fit. From there we began our two-year affair.

On the other hand, Marianne had let herself go. I wanted her to get fit and work out again. I hated it when Marianne said if you love me you won't care if I put on a little weight. Wrong. Before, her beautiful full figure and breasts kept me interested. Still, guys like Jim and Henry thought she was good looking.

— — —

Abby was always growing intellectually and artistically. She would go to galleries and museums in the area. Marianne would talk about doing the things Abby was doing but it was empty talk. It was fake like most of the people in society today. All pseudo. Recently, in an article I was writing, I talked about Thomas Merton and how he described those early Christians in the wilderness as people who did not believe in letting themselves be passively guided and formed by a decadent state—as people who didn't wish to be ruled or to rule. He goes on to say that people primarily had to seek their true self in Christ; to do so, they had to reject the false formal self that was fabricated under the social compulsion in the world. If they sought a way to God, it had to be uncharted and freely chosen, not inherited from others who had mapped it out beforehand.

Several years ago I wrote an article that was titled "An Educator in Exile." In the midst of what was happening with me and Abby, and Marianne's depression, my chairman, Neil, called me in and said that the president of Cayuga College felt that the article was full of humanistic jargon. The president told Neil he knows something about literature. He had an undergraduate degree in it from Colgate. Neil said that the president mentioned I should write an article on how Dickens adapts and transforms conventions of the eighteenth-century past on to an urban environment. He also said he wrote a paper once on Dickens's use of fairly tales. That's the stuff, he went on to say, I should write about—not the simple, non-scholarly humanistic or human potential bullshit that I was writing. And I thought, why was the president now interested in an article I wrote several years ago? What was going on?

In short, I didn't know what the fucking president was talking about. I heard he hardly read, because most of his time was spent on fundraising. I remembered in that article, I wrote that the education structure has lost meaning for me. The "cult of efficiency" is what is winning higher ed, and it is winning badly. Also, I remembered writing that educators like me, who are in exile, sense that our only hope is to journey beyond the dead models of literature. If not, we can perhaps for the first time envision the dismantling of literature education as we presently know it. As Sven Birkerts argues in his book *The Guttenberg Elegies*, we must be careful in our new technological information society that we don't lose the ability to think deeply and critically. I needed to see the president and articulate and clarify my positions I took in that article.

— — —

Freddy, the night Marianne went missing I drank a bottle of wine and passed out on the sofa. I dreamed about Marianne being a crow and was pecking me to death. My cell phone then began ringing and ringing. I saw on the phone it was 3:51 in the morning.

"Yes," I answered, not knowing if the crow was still pecking.

"Paul, it's Rose."

"What's wrong?" I asked in a voiced that seemed so far away.

"I got a text from Marianne around two this morning. She said that she needed clarity in her life. She doesn't like the direction your marriage was going. What does she mean, Paul?"

"I don't know," I lied. "I just know that she has not been herself these past several months. Everything seemed to be bothering her. Me, the kids, I don't know, at times she seemed more depressed than ever."

"Should we call the police?" She asked, crying.

"Let's wait. It's too early for them to get involved."

"Okay. Bill is really worried. So are the kids."

"I understand. I'll stop over later today and see how they are doing. Do you want me to take them home?"

"No, they're fine. We enjoy having them around. It keeps our minds occupied while Marianne is missing. You just work on finding Marianne."

"I'll do that. First I'll call her friends Carol and Jennifer. Maybe they know something," I lied.

"We tried calling them last night, but we got no answer."

"Look, Rose, she may still be in town, and not on the road. Last night I checked out all our hangouts like the Sherwood, Blue Moon, Rosalie's, and others. No one had seen her."

"Call if you hear anything."

I hung up and thought about what I would tell Marianne if she comes back. Perhaps I'll just tell her Abby is a student of mine, and she invited me and some others to get some concepts straight about James Joyce's work. I don't know if she'll believe me given that time at the fitness center when she caught me helping out a student by the name of Bonnie. I remembered thinking the student looked like a young Natalie Wood. I think she was falling in love with me.

Anyway, as I was standing over Bonnie's stomach pulling her weights off, I remembered, just then I felt a punch in the back. I looked around and it was Marianne.

Angrily, she asked, "Who's this?"

"Just a student of mine who needed help."

"I bet," she said sarcastically. She turned and left while Bonnie lay on the mat stunned.

I tried calling Bonnie afterwards but was told by her roommate she was unavailable to talk to me. I don't know why, perhaps she was mad about Marianne or maybe I showed her too much affection by touching her arm and leaving it there too long.

I wanted to tell Bonnie, if I talked to her more, that the other women at the fitness center were always hitting on me. There is a word that maybe describes my condition. I just can't remember it now. But I know that it's about thinking all the time women are falling in love with you, but they're not. *Erotomania*, that's the word.

– – –

A few years ago, Freddy, I had a heart attack. That's why I'm so obsessed about working out. I don't want it to happen again. I must be honest here. Marianne was a great nurse while I recovered from the operation. I think I'm a fairly good-looking fortyish male—tall, grayish hair, and a somewhat slender body from years of watching what I eat and also jogging daily. In fact, the doctor said that because I was a jogger all my life, it helped the blood get around the blocked arteries.

I also told the doctor about blacking out at different times of stress. And that I always thought it was maybe due to epileptic seizures that were never diagnosed. The doctor doubted that, he told me the blackouts were due to what he called *syncope*. This type of blackout is caused by a problem in the regulation of blood pressure, which also affects the heart.

I used to jog with Marianne when we first got married, but because of our busy schedules now we hardly ran together anymore. I don't know. I just felt she just wanted to be alone in her running.

– – –

## Looking for Marianne

Our home was on East Genesee Street in Skaneateles. It was a beautiful two-story home with white siding and blue shutters on the windows. After I got back from Shirley's, I decided that night I would walk down to the Sherwood, which was on the same street.

As I walked through the downtown area, I thought how charming Skaneateles was with its small clothing boutiques and art galleries. People came from all over to shop, eat, and sit at the lake. Of course, the rich loved its uniqueness along with many celebrities, like Tom Cruise, newscaster David Muir, who was from nearby Port Byron, Richard Gere, Alex Baldwin and his brothers, and several others. In fact, the Clintons used to come to Skaneateles with all their political friends. It seemed throughout the country Skaneateles was well known for its wealth and celebrityhood.

– – –

Once I got to the Sherwood, I thought of its history, that at one time in the 1800s it was where stagecoaches stopped for passengers to eat and sleep. Full of history.

As I sat at the bar wondering and thinking, *Where are you Marianne? Will you ever come back? I've got to call the police first thing tomorrow.* But now I needed a glass of wine. I got myself a huge glass in a paper cup and walked across street, sat on a park bench, and gazed at the lake as a gentle breeze moved across it and, like a mirror, reflected the oak trees above with the moon beginning to shine on it. Skaneateles means "beautiful squaw" in the Onondaga Native American language. When I jogged around the lake, I loved the mornings as the fog lifted like a curtain and revealed the beautiful bluish-green color.

Ping. It was a text from Marianne:

*"How many women, or students I should say, have you screwed over the years? Thousands?"*

– – –

The next morning at seven I called the police. They said they would be at my house in a couple of hours. Soon after I hung up, I felt hot and found it very difficult to breathe. Then quickly I took an Ativan and began doing some deep breathing exercises I learned in cardiac rehab. In a few moments I was feeling better and began to think what I was going to tell the police.

Around nine the doorbell rang over and over. I ran downstairs quickly and opened the door. Two men were standing there, flashing their badges. One was tall, thin, and balding. He wore a fake smile like the other one who was short and fat. Their suits were black and wrinkled.

I said, "Come in." Then, I led them to the living room. They both sat on the sofa, which had roses splattered here and there on a cream-colored background. I sat in a light-blue wing chair across from them. Our house was decorated in early colonial. Marianne's choice, not mine. I would've preferred more modern. The tall one spoke first.

"Mister Testa, and am I saying it right?"

"Yes."

"This shouldn't take very long."

"Okay." I tried hard looking sad and depressed.

"Well," he continued, "when did you notice your wife missing?"

"When I came home two nights ago she wasn't here. Her mother called and said that she dropped the kids off. Marianne told her she just had to get away for a while. And that's it. Her mother said she got a text from her later, and it just said something about she needed more time to think."

The short policeman asked, "Were you and Mrs. Testa having problems?"

"Not really, you know, just the normal things like why do I work all the time and how come you didn't bring out the garbage. Just normal things married couples fight about. You know what I mean?"

"Yes," the tall one answered. "Well, that's all we need for now. Here's our cards." He handed me two business cards.

"Also," he said, "we really can't do anything legally until she's been missing at least three days. It's been only two now."

"I understand."

Then both got up and left. I noticed about three or four TV trucks were now parked in front of the house. Who would've called and told them?

Glancing at the business cards, I noticed that one detective was named Harrison, I think he was the tall one. The other's name was Kohl, the fat one, I think.

Right after, I decided to go over and see Jake and Sara. I missed them. But why don't I feel anything about Marianne gone missing? I drove over to Bill and Rose's on the west side of the lake. They had a beautiful two-story, white brick home. When I got there, both Jake and Sara came out to greet me. I loved them so much. First, I gave Jake a big hug and then Sara. Sara was blossoming into a beautiful girl just like her mother. She was twelve and Jake was eleven. Together we walked into the house with arms around each other. We went into the dining room where I could see they had been eating breakfast. They went back to their seats and continued eating.

Rose asked, "Do you want anything, Paul?"

"No, I'm fine," I said.

Sara asked, "What about Mommy?"

"Don't worry, she'll be home soon."

Behind me, I heard Rose say, "Yeah, she'll be okay. She just needed a little break."

Bill, who was sitting at the head of the table, said nothing. He smiled sadly at me.

"Are you guys okay?" I said in the direction of Jake and Sara.

"Yes, we like it here with Grandpa and Grandma."

"Well, if you guys need anything, just let Daddy know. I'm going to be spending time today looking for Mommy."

"Okay," they both said affectionately.

Rose and Bill motioned for me to follow them into the fully modern kitchen. Once inside, Rose spoke first. "Did you see the police?"

"I saw them this morning."

"What did they say?" Bill asked, worried.

"They can't do anything until she's been missing for at least three days. Anyway, I'm going to start looking today. And you guys can start calling around."

"We will," Rose said. "We'll organize search parties if she isn't back soon."

"The media already knows," I said. "They were in front of my house this morning and I see they're coming around here. Looks like around four TV trucks are out in front of your house."

"Yeah, we noticed that too," Rose said. "It's because all those people like Tom Cruise hang around at that new Mirbeau Spa. And, of course, those people love to eat at that great Italian restaurant, Rosalie's."

Without expecting it, Rose gave me a hug while Bill shook my hand and said, "Whatever we can do to help, let us know, Paul."

"We love you, Paul." Rose said, crying. "I want my daughter home." She then released her tight hug.

"So do I, Rose, so do I," I said with as much sadness as I could conjure up.

After talking with Jake and Sara again about Marianne and that everything will be fine, I said, "Be strong," as I kissed and hugged them goodbye.

On the way to get into my car, I noticed even more TV trucks driving up.

Immediately I drove over to Abby's place. I needed to see her, even though it was still morning.

We had been spending more and more time together—either after class, in my office, or at her place.

To think, we had been lovers for almost two years now. I could sense other students were jealous of the attention I gave her in class but I didn't care. I have fallen in love with her. She was bright, articulate, kind, and gentle. Her love was exceptional. With the other girls it wasn't the same. Over two years, she had taken four classes with me.

There was now a ping. It was a text from Marianne. I stopped the car in front of Abby's condo and read:

*When I'm done with you no one will ever believe you. You know, Paul, one time when I came downstairs I heard you in your study with the door closed. You were saying something, about rubbing, rubbing ... what the fuck was that? How old was she? Eighteen? Nineteen? Another night I heard you saying that you couldn't make it to the hotel in Rochester because your son was sick. Paul, you're a sick puppy. Were you having phone sex?*

I worried that if Marianne didn't come back I'd be a suspect. The husband is always the first suspect. Then I thought of Phyllis, a woman I met and what happened to her. You remember. Freddy, they brought her up at the trial and the police asked about her early on, but now I want to give you the full story. It happened when I was rehabilitating from my heart attack.

A colleague of mine in the English Department by the name of Janet Powers told me about Phyllis. Janet was a tiny woman with a gray pixie haircut and a small, unusually narrow face with big blue eyes. One day she stopped by my office at Cayuga and said she wanted me to meet a friend of hers, by the name of Phyllis Charles, and Phyllis's daughter. Janet then went on to say that the daughter wanted to be a model. Janet knew that every so often I modeled for an agency in Syracuse. I was used mostly for modeling ads for prostate pills and Polo ads for Macy's.

Anyway, I told Janet I would meet Phyllis and her daughter at a small coffee shop just down from my house. In a way, I was glad to get out of the house. Marianne and the kids said I was driving them crazy

— — —

When I walked into the coffee shop I saw this woman perhaps in her mid-forties, and a young girl sitting in the back. The woman waved me over. Smiling I shook their hands as I sat down. She was a pretty woman with long legs stretched underneath the table and had flowing brunette hair cupping her narrow face. Her daughter had sandy blonde hair, huge brown eyes, and a thin body. Her clothes hung on her. She seemed lost, as Phyllis did most of the talking. "I appreciate you taking the time to see us, Professor," she said.

"Please call me Paul."

"Okay," she said reluctantly. "You see, Prof—I mean Paul, my daughter here, Ariel, loves to dress up in a new outfit every day," she smiled again as she brushed her hair back from her face. Her move was sexy. "Paul, I also write but only have a GED. An English teacher friend of mine said I was pretty good."

"That's good." I think she was more interested in talking about herself than her daughter's modeling career.

"I've been writing for a long time, but I don't know how at times to put sentences together. You know what I mean?"

"Yes."

"I have a lot of thoughts about caskets and an old man with a white beard standing near my bed." There was a quaver in her voice.

Her daughter was not listening to her mother and suddenly interrupted and said, "I just like dressing up." She seemed very determined to let me know that. She was a junior at East High in Skaneateles.

"Look," I said, "Ariel, why don't you email me some of your photos? And also your mom can send some of her writings. Okay?"

"Thank you, thank you," her mom said happily. Phyllis was not overly built but seemed to be designed for speed and endurance. As she kept flipping her hair from her face, I noticed she seemed jittery and vulnerable.

And, Freddy, I should've told you more about Holly from the fitness center as you were getting ready for the trial. I felt so bad that you just heard of her during the trial. Sorry, I'll explain later on.

"Thank you," I heard Phyllis now saying again, happily.

Later that night I opened my tablet and saw an email from Phyllis with two attachments. First I opened the PDF with Ariel's photos. I felt that they made her look cheap and anorexic. Then I opened the PDF with Phyllis's writings. Her writing seemed raw and troubling. I needed to study it more so I took the tablet off the dining room table and went out to the front porch with a glass of wine.

I turned on the tablet again as a pain in my chest began. I now saw an email from the modeling agency that I contacted earlier, saying that they were not taking anyone Ariel's age because they had too many in her age category. Then I clicked into Phyllis's writings again.

*She grew weary with the fear of the constant anger and arguing among her parents in which she knew that he was going to beat her after he beat her mother. Anytime they got into an argument he would stammer up the stairs and angrily scream out her name, "Amanda," and say, "You can't hide from me …."*

Her story went on and on about how Amanda's father, who was a preacher, would beat her over and over because he said she had "evil eyes." The church people thought she was possessed. He thought he must cleanse her before she could be accepted.

> *In bed, she slightly rolled her head to the right side of her body and catches a glimpse of a black shadowy figure hovering over her. This thing is on her and peering down and hurts her. She is in utter terror as she releases a huge scream. He quickly leaves through the window and into the fog and this is where her pain begins ... She is gripped with utter fear and tried to yell out for help but she couldn't get out any more sounds ....*

I took a nitroglycerin along with the wine, and it helped my chest pain to subside for a while. Back to Phyllis, I wondered how many more times she was physically or even sexually abused. *What about the daughter?* I asked. I lay down the tablet and drank some more wine. I wanted to connect to them for it might help me forget my pain. I blamed Marianne for my looking around. After our children were born she got more depressed. And then she always found an excuse to not have sex: food poisoning, sinuses, too tired, migraine headaches, and on and on it went. In fact, after a while we couldn't make serious eye contact for we knew our marriage was in trouble. We used euphemisms like "I missed you today" and "I love you." But it was all a lie, and yet we stayed married because of the kids.

I drank excessively sometimes to deal with the pain of living with someone I didn't love anymore. The end result for me was having a major heart attack. Of course, my fooling around with students didn't help. That was a major stressor.

I turned on the tablet again, and I began to read more of Phyllis's writings.

> *Slowly the lids of the caskets opened up, there lying in the caskets were her mom, dad, her two brothers and her two sisters .... An empty casket came to Amanda, floating around her, she knew what it was wanting. She leaped upon the casket and it started taking her through the tunnel of fire ... Going further in the tunnel, she saw that skeletons were forming on the walls of the tunnel. They were falling all around her, an arm, then a leg, the bones kept falling .... Then water starts to push her upward. She loses her hold of her casket and tumbles out ....*

In a sense, Phyllis had some structural problems with her writings, but she had an abused voice that needed to be heard. Soon afterwards, I called Phyllis and told her I wanted to meet her for lunch the next day at the same coffeehouse. She agreed to meet me and said her daughter could not be there because of cheerleading.

When we met, she was wearing a tweed suit with a black sweater underneath. I asked her if she worked and she said she had been a personal trainer for over twenty years. Now I understood why she had such a good-looking figure. Today, I noticed she seemed again very nervous. She was talking and going in many different directions at the same time.

"Hey, Phyllis, what's wrong?" I asked.

"Nothing," she said.

"Are you sure?"

"Well, I was worried about what you would think about my crazy writing." Tears welled up in her eyes as our glasses of *Revolutionary* red wine came. It was the only wine I drank now.

"What is it?" I asked. I wanted to hug her because she seemed so sad.

However, she spoke with more clarity now. "You know I have never dealt with why I got married at sixteen. I hide myself in the corners of my house because of him. My mother and father live with us."

"You mean your dad? Did he sexually abuse you?"

"I don't know," she cried a little. "I just know I'm weary of hiding. Really, I view others as figments of my imagination and they scare the hell out of me. I avoid conflict and friendship like the plague. You know, come to think of it, it was sort of sexual abuse," she said with more control in her voice. "But it wasn't just my father. I was in Ohio and you know how kids are. My girlfriend and I were running all over the place. Our parents didn't care. It was a rock concert. Then these guys got us drinking and they raped us over and over. People think after being raped you are just a victim. But life goes on after, you know?" Tears began to well up even more in her eyes, reflecting the sunlight from the outside.

For a long while, Phyllis said nothing—just nothing. With innocence and reserve, she gave off this feeling of an intense "something" concealed in her.

"I will no longer," she now said, "be silent, keeping it hidden and shameful. I want to empower others to come forward. Still, I don't know. Sometimes I talk a good game, but like now I'm trembling inside and I want to die."

Again, I wanted to hug her and tell her I knew what she's going through. My chest pain was starting up again.

"Tell me, what do you really want to do with your life? You can't hide all the time."

"I want to write and help young people with their pain. I hate hearing about them killing themselves because of being abused or molested."

Then she started changing the subject every few minutes. We went from suicide, to rape, Jesus, her days living in Amish country, Ariel, Ariel's clothes, and so on.

Finally, I asked, "Amanda, in the story, that's really you, right?"

"Yes," she said weakly.

"Have you had therapy?" I asked.

"Yes, but I never told the truth. Most of those guys are jerks."

"If you want to tell your story, you have to tell them the truth," I said.

"I will, if it will help the kids. I found Ariel with a bottle of pills last week. Maybe it's in her DNA because

## Looking for Marianne

I was hooked on them for a long time, Paul. Maybe it's wrong, but I'm trying to understand life. Help me Paul, to understand."

My heart pain was getting really intense now. I sneaked a nitroglycerin into my mouth. It helped a little.

I told her I had to get back home because I was expecting a call from my publisher. I lie so easily.

On the way out of the coffee shop I told Phyllis that I would help her with her writing. I went on that her writing needed work. However, something in her writing intrigued me.

"Thank you for being willing to help. You are becoming my mentor and leader," she said.

"I don't know. I doubt it," I said.

She touched my shoulder, we headed in opposite directions. There was something good about her, but also something dark looming over her.

Turning her head back to me, she said, "I'll text you tonight."

"Okay," I said. The pain in my chest was really intense now. I needed some wine and pain pills. Even though neither of us had been in the service, she, like me, perhaps had PTSD. Hers was from abuse, and mine was from a marriage that had very little love in it.

That night I called Phyllis and we went for a drive. We met in the front of the Sherwood. I drove on Route 41 for a few miles and then we parked on an overlook as moonbeams bounced off the lake. She asked me to just hold her tight as she cried into my chest. It felt good for once in my life to hold someone without eventually making love. Later, I dropped her off in front of the Sherwood and promised to call her tomorrow. She could be a good friend. Right now, I was too centered on my life; now was a time to center on another life. Perhaps I could even help her daughter.

When I got home, I thought, *What a beautiful night*. There was a bright, nearly full moon, a gentle breeze, the twinkling in the deep black sky, and the smell of nearby lake wineries. For now, total relaxation and peace and almost no pain. My sleep that night came without pills and wine.

In a half dream state, I thought I answered the phone, but I couldn't remember. Dazed, I thought it was Phyllis and she wanted me to meet her again—at Glen Haven, right now. She apologized for being late. Glen Haven was a once-famous resort on the lake that celebrities would come to in order to be cured of their illnesses by the cool waters of Skaneateles. Several years ago, it went bankrupt and what was left was a restaurant in the style of a café. All I could remember was being in a deep sleep and not going anywhere.

The next morning, feeling refreshed, I slipped on my sweats and pulled a gray Cayuga College sweatshirt over my head. Then I prepared the Keurig for coffee and, coffee cup in hand, went out on the porch. I loved the silence of early mornings when Marianne and the kids were over at her parents'. My cell then rang.

"Hi," I answered.

"Paul, this is Janet. Have you heard?" She seemed to be out of breath.

"What?" I asked her.

"Phyllis shot her husband and children last night and then herself."

Shaking uncontrollably now, I dropped the phone, with my mind turned off, I only saw the stark whiteness. I wanted to be back in time before the phone call. *Take me back, God.*

– – –

As I now walked to Abby's front door, I still wondered why Phyllis did what she did. Was I the reason she did it? *No*, I thought, *she seemed to have so many other problems*.

Every once in a while, I get pain in my chest but for the most part it's gone since meeting Abby. And again, why am I not feeling anything about Marianne missing.

I opened the door and called up to Abby and she called down and told me to come up. Hurriedly, I ran up the stairs, dropped my briefcase, which I carried anytime I came over. I wanted Marianne or anyone else who saw me to think I was meeting a colleague from the college. Another lie. Once I kissed Abby, my mind was on her and what we would do. Riverdale and Aaron, chest pain, Phyllis, and the police all vanished from my mind. She handed me a glass of wine as I sat on the sofa with her. It was too early for wine but I needed it. Every once in a while I thought I was alcoholic.

"Have you heard from Marianne?"

"No," I said. "The police were over yesterday morning."

"What did they ask?"

"Nothing, they just wanted to know how long she was gone and if we were having any problems."

"What did you say?"

"I said everything was okay."

"Of course, we both know that's not true," she said.

"I know, but what else am I going to say?"

"I know, honey, I just feel bad that perhaps, we caused all of this."

"Look, Abby, this has been coming for years." I touched her back, her hair, and then kissed her hair. I now slowly unbuttoned her blouse and then turned her gently around to me and unfastened her bra. Slowly, I traced my fingers across her breasts. I could feel an excited heat flow from her breasts to my fingers and that heat was stronger as I touched her thighs. As I pulled her down on the sofa, I saw the moon peeking in on us through her living room window. She moaned with pleasure. My wandering fingers seem to take on a magical touch as her body arched toward me.

"I love you, Paul."

"So do I."

Afterwards, Abby said, "Oh, Paul, I got a call yesterday from a girl named Holly Adams. She said she wanted to talk to me about what you did to her. And she said you're doing the same thing to me. She hoped we could talk. Do you know her? She really sounded upset at you."

"I don't know," I said. "I may have met her at the fitness center. She's about fifteen and goes to Skaneateles High, I think. She seemed to be an emotionally troubled girl."

– – –

Now it was getting serious. For what seemed like too long, I haven't heard anything from Marianne. No texts, no phone calls, nothing at all for four days. I wondered what Harrison and Kohl were doing. This case means they have to work. Normally they perhaps sit around all day doing very little except getting called out for fender benders.

Later on the fourth day, Rose called and she said more media trucks and reporters were all over her front yard. Skaneateles was in the national news now. The real estate agents were happy because the media would always bring up the celebrities that lived there.

Nervously, Rose said, "Paul, we need to do something."

"What?" I asked.

"Bill and I think we should go on TV and tell the community about Marianne and how much we miss her and that we need their help. You need to be here."

"Okay," I said. Sometimes I thought I came across with no affect. I need to work on that.

She went on to say, "I hate it, but we have to really form search parties now. Carol and Jennifer are willing to help." I wondered how Carol and Jennifer found out.

"Okay, whatever you think. How are Jake and Sara?"

"I can see they are worried," Rose said.

"Listen, Rose, I want to thank you and Bill for watching the kids. I'm, completely out of it."

"That's fine. However, do you mind, Paul, that Bill and I are sort of doing the coordinating?"

"No, that's fine. It's time for that."

"Good," she said, almost relieved.

– – –

The next day, the fifth day Marianne was missing, Harrison called and said he and Kohl wanted to see me at the station today around noon. When I arrived, my first ever time there, I realized that the police station was an old high school called West High School, as indicated by the old lettering cast in the cement archway over the entrance. In the building's rear, I assumed, was the jail. It was all cement blocks with a few barred windows.

Harrison led me up to the second floor where there seemed to be a series of interrogation rooms. We went into one, which was painted yellow and fading. The walls also had some indentations, where it looked like people had hit the walls with their fists.

Harrison directed me to a chair behind a worn, black table. He sat opposite me. Across from me was a huge window where I know Detective Kohl was standing.

"Well, how are you doing Mr. Testa?" Harrison asked in a fake friendly voice.

"Okay, I guess."

"Today marks the fifth day your wife has been missing."

"I know."

"Have you heard from her?"

"No," I lied.

"So, you wouldn't know any place she might be?"

"No."

"Now, she was driving a 2012 Honda CRV. It was gray, right?"

"Yes."

"We talked to your in-laws and they're also in the dark."

"Yes, I know."

"They told us they're making posters, and she and her husband and Marianne's friends are going to start looking around both sides of the lake."

"Yes, I know. I plan to help," I said, fake sobbing a little.

"Again, Mr. Testa, you said your marriage was okay except for normal husband and wife disagreements, right?"

"Yeah, I just don't know. She has never done anything like this before."

"Was she having mental health problems? I mean, was she seeing a therapist?"

"God, no," I lied.

"Do you know Phyllis Charles?"

"Yes, I was trying to help her daughter get into modeling. I can't believe what happened."

"Well, we heard that you were having an affair with her."

"My God, I only met her once. You can ask my colleague Janet Powers at Cayuga College."

*How the hell did they find out about Phyllis?* I thought.

Harrison stood up. "Look Mr. Testa, that's all we have for you today."

I stood up also.

"Okay, thanks."

And just before we got to the door, Harrison asked, "Paul, are you sure you didn't have anything to do with your wife's disappearance?"

"Yes, I'm sure," I said strongly.

As I drove home I was still worried how they found out about Phyllis. Anyway, I had my gym clothes in the car and decided to go to the fitness center for a while. It would be nice to see if Abby was there. Once inside there didn't seem to be too many people working out. I didn't see Abby around. There was a girl with long blonde hair on a treadmill. I went over and grabbed an empty one next to her.

"Hi," she said friendly like.

"Hi," I said, thinking to myself, *I can't move on her because I think the police are now watching my every move.*

"Are you the guy, that the wife is missing?"

"Yes," I said, "How did you know?"

"Someone said something the other day when you were here. And I've seen you on TV."

"Oh, I see." I thought, *Paul, you have to be very careful getting together with Abby now. They're watching. My privacy is gone. Don't fuck around, Paul.* I know the girl at the fitness center wanted to talk more but I couldn't. Once we get the stuff with Marianne settled, I can get to know the girl next to me better.

– – –

Some days, when my mother was off visiting one of her friends, she would say, "I'll be back in an hour." That really meant three hours. I knew she would eventually come home, but I still worried that maybe she left for good. I was afraid of being left alone forever.

Even though Marianne and I were growing apart, I sort of felt the same way when Marianne went missing. She would never come back and I would be left alone. Aloneness was my greatest fear. Yes, I had Abby but she could tire of me, and again, I would be alone.

I bet Marianne is in New York City. Lost for good amidst the millions of people.

Freddy, as you know, I loved the City. Marianne felt the same way at one time. In fact, she interned at the Museum of Modern Art while she was an undergraduate at Wellesley College in Massachusetts. She told me everything in the city—the noise, the traffic and

## Looking for Marianne

crowds—gave her anonymity. She needed that then, and perhaps now because of my philandering and her state of depression. She told me she hated the City.

*Damn, Marianne, where are you?*

— — —

After going to the fitness center for a while I went over to Bill and Rose's house around mid-afternoon. There seemed to be now hundreds of people in the front carrying posters with Marianne's picture on it. Ahead of me, I saw Bill and Rose being interviewed as they motioned for me to come over. Walking toward them, people kept coming up to me saying they were sorry and if they could do anything to help. *Look*, I wanted to say, *she's not dead. She'll be back soon. I'm not that guy Scott Peterson who killed his wife in California.* Eventually, I know the police will start saying I am perhaps a suspect.

Now a skinny-assed reporter who was interviewing Bill and Rose saw me and quickly stuck a mic in my face. Another person had a camera on me.

"I'm sorry Mr. Testa, I know this is a difficult time for you. Do you have an idea of what happened to your wife?" The reporter asked.

"No, I hope she comes back soon. The children and I miss her. We love you, honey," I said as I looked straight into the camera. "Anyone that has seen her, please call the police. I also appreciate all the people who want to help. Marianne, please come home. Sorry but now I have to go inside and pick up my kids." Promptly, I moved away from the skinny-ass reporter and camera.

Rose yelled after me, "Paul, do you want something to eat?"

"No, I'm fine. I'll get something with the kids. They love the Chicken McNuggets from McDonald's."

"It's good you're going to be with Jake and Sara," Rose said. "They miss their mom and dad."

"I know."

"We're going with the group that's searching the east side of the lake," she said.

"Good."

– – –

Freddy, I hope you're still with me. But for now, I want to talk to you about the fitness center. It was my thing because I liked meeting new people, especially good looking women and girls. And I also loved working out. On the other hand, Marianne loved running outside. She also loved running 10K and 25K races. She said that running helped reduce her depression, though I noticed she wasn't running as often now.

A couple weeks ago, she was talking with me about what she was reading by Heather Armstrong in her book, *The Valedictorian of Being Dead: The True Story of Dying Ten Times to Live*.

She said the author was cured of her depression by sort of being put to death over and over by the same drug that Michael Jackson took before he died. I guess, according to her, the depressed woman died almost ten times, which froze the depression cells in her brain and eventually she lost her depression. The only problem, Marianne said, with the drug was the side effects. The main side effect was it gave you unbelievable migraines, and Marianne hated any kind of headache. When she felt one coming on she would pop an Advil as soon as possible.

– – –

That night, I got a text from Marianne. This time, a really long one. Marianne's just about the only person I know who does really long texts.

*I heard the people are having search parties for me. God, I miss the kids. You know, the first seven years of our life was good. The kids were so precious then. I was proud to be your wife. You were good looking, witty, and brilliant. It seemed you knew everything. When we went out with our few friends, you owned the conversation. I added a little. It seemed after our last child was born, Jake, we started to drift apart and my depression got worse. You were always having these faculty meetings at night. That's when I started to think maybe you were going out on me. We hadn't had sex in months, years? And if we did, you just went through the motions. That's why that one night I couldn't stand to be rejected again, so, I know it was terrible. I don't care now. I wished you'd died. You went unconscious. I did think I killed you, but you son-of-a-bitch, you woke up. Now I know all those so-called faculty meetings were lies. You were fucking that little bitch and others.*

*When we were first married you always asked me to give you feedback on the books and articles you wrote. You stopped doing that a few years ago. Even though I have a master's degree in English from Rochester and an undergraduate degree from Wellesley. After a while, you never asked. I just might kill myself so the police will blame you and you'll be put away for life. Who will you fuck then, Paul, your prison bunkmate? You know someday I will die soon. I felt I have been dying all my life. I know I have a disease that kills over time.*

– – –

The sixth day I was with a search party that was walking through a vineyard on the west side of the lake. The name of the vineyard was Anyela's. When things were good between us, Marianne and I spent many late afternoons there drinking their Overlay wine, which had the right balance of spices here and there. The view from where we sat on Anyela's patio was spectacular, with lusty green vineyards below and even further down the silver-like Skaneateles Lake created by the descending sun. Sometime the sky would turn violet and rose, especially before a major rainstorm. In the late fall, you would see Anyela's workers starting to bury the vines so that the Central New York winters would not kill them.

I thought, as I walked along with the search party, with the crisp cold of the mornings now and the partial remaining leaves on the trees, soon the first flakes will be here.

The search party was now spreading out like we were preparing for battle in the Civil War. And I continued to respond with a smile to all those search party people who came by to say they were sorry about Marianne missing. "Thank you, thank you, thank you ..." My jaws hurt from giving them my fake smile over and over again.

After about two hours the search party came up empty! *Marianne is gone and gone for good,* I thought. As I drove back now to the village of Skaneateles, I thought about my parents and what they would think about Marianne missing. My father wouldn't care, for he always thought Marianne was too arrogant and uppity. Little did he know, she hated him because my mother had told her about all his women. You see, Freddy, when my mother was well she and Marianne were like the best of friends. They would go shopping almost every week. Marianne also knew about the rumor that Paul's father's stores were backed by the mafia out of Buffalo. When the financial crisis hit in 2008, my mother told me that my father couldn't pay the mafia back what he borrowed so they pressured him so much the end result was his stroke and his death.

Today my mother lives in an assisted living facility just outside of Skaneateles. It's called Our Lady of Sorrows.

I try to visit her at least once a month, and the last time I was with her, I saw the beginning stages of Alzheimer's taking its toll. She asked me if I liked being a priest at St. Anne's. Thank God she has that trust money from her parents, because I couldn't pay for her care now that I'm almost broke.

When my father was home, he drank a lot, especially homemade red wine. Also, he had an uncontrollable anger. The littlest things would set him off. One time he was home, drunk, and I spilled some milk on the floor. Full of anger, he chased me up to my bedroom, caught me and threw me on the bed. With clenched fists, he hit me over and over. I was black and blue on my chest, arms, and legs for months.

On the other hand, my father never hit my mother, but he loved to verbally abuse her. His favorite words for her were, "Stupid, lazy bastard."

A funny thing I could never figure out, he cried like a baby if he was home and I was leaving for Riverdale or Harvard. On the other hand, any time I was home on vacation from Riverdale or Harvard, he had me working at one of his stores. He said I read too much and I needed to know what it was like to do hard labor eight or ten hours a day. *We don't choose our fathers*.

My mother would say that I had my father's good looks, but also his kind and caring ways when he wasn't drinking. I remembered how proud of me he was when he introduced me to his employees, especially when I was at Harvard. Still I thought my mother loved him regardless of how mean he treated her. There was a day I remembered from when I was younger. He kissed her as he shoved her against a house wall and cupped her breasts with his powerful hands. And I also always heard lovemaking noises coming from their bedroom.

– – –

As I was now walking up the sidewalk to my house, I heard a horn beeping. It was Harrison in his car, rolling down his window and asking, "Paul, can you come down to the office for a few more things? Tomorrow at ten, okay?"

"Okay," I said. I knew they were trying to book me. Damn Marianne!

– – –

Freddy, I wish you could have been with me when both Harrison and Kohl led me into the same windowless interrogation room as before.

As we sat down, Harrison asked, "Paul, you okay, buddy?"

"The best you could expect, considering the circumstance."

"Look, we notified all the Sheriff Departments and Troopers in the state. We're trying, Paul."

"I know."

Kohl then said, "Paul, we just need you to sign some of these papers to give us permission to look at your credit cards, phone records, and all the stuff that could end up helping you and us in the end."

"I know," I said. "Guys, I understand, the husband is the prime suspect. But let me be clear, I didn't do anything. She went away on her own."

Harrison, now in a serious and suspecting voice, asked, "Where were you that night she disappeared?"

"I was working out at the fitness center."

Harrison got up and said, "Okay. You can go now."

– – –

I left the station, thinking I'd get to see Abby tonight—so we're all on the same page. This is so TV-ish, like *Dateline* and *20/20*.

I thought I should go back to the search area, then I figured I should go over to Abby's before anywhere else. No, it's too early. I know the police are watching me. It was starting to rain and getting dreary outside.

Finally, I decided to go over to Bill and Rose's house again, which had become the center for the search parties. People have been bringing over food and cookies now every day.

Today the search parties were going out on Route 20 where several apple orchards were located. It was pouring rain now.

Up behind me, I heard a voice say, "Paul, I want to help." I saw, when I turned around, that it was Snake Bevin, a sort of a friend. He was a guy I knew from St. Boniface Elementary. I don't know why he was called Snake. He was a big guy with an angled face, with little hair on his head. I think he was a pharmaceutical rep now. He must've heard about Marianne being missing from the Syracuse media. I'm sure he still lived there.

"How can I help?" he asked.

"Well, if you go over to one of those tables near the front of the house, someone will take care of you. I don't know how much we'll get done today because of the rain. Anyway, they got food. Good seeing you again, buddy, thanks for helping."

"I remember meeting Marianne at your wedding. Man, I thought she was beautiful."

"Thanks."

Just then some older ladies came over. They were all dressed in yellow rain gear and boots. Usually Marianne and I would see them when we went to the Sherwood Inn. If they had husbands with them, the men usually all looked half-dazed, with dementia or from having had a stroke, while the women looked vibrant and unusually healthy.

One woman with a huge, floppy rain hat asked, "Paul, you doing okay?"

"Yes, I'm doing okay."

"Look," she said, "my husband died last year so I would love the company if you would want to just talk. My name is Darlene Patterson."

"I'll do that but I got too much other stuff now going on, you understand?"

"Yes," she said, sadly.

I saw that Snake was over at the food table while this woman Darlene was still in front of me and I thought shit, she was hitting on me. She smiled seductively as she stroked and held my arm in a flirtatious manner.

I smiled at her, pulled my arm away, and hurriedly caught up with the group that was heading out to Route 20. The rain had almost stopped.

– – –

Ping, another text from Marianne:

*You know I could never tell you this before because you and society would consider it an illicit lover. But it isn't. This person is my best friend and has wallpapered my total life with love. And I want you to know that there was no way you could compete with this person. I only met her a few months ago, and I love her so much.*

– – –

Freddy, I think I told you already that I met Marianne at the University of Rochester while I was working on my PhD in English literature. She was working on her master's in the same area. A friend of mine, Bob Hole, fixed me up with her on a blind date. Immediately, I knew she was the one I wanted to marry. She was beautiful, smart, sexy, and great in bed. We loved going out to eat and then dancing until we almost passed out with exhaustion. She had everything I was looking for in a wife.

After we received our degrees, we got married and moved to Skaneateles, because we both loved the area. The lake was jewel-clear. The panoramic views from the surrounding hills were beautiful. Most importantly, Marianne's parents had bought a lovely big home on the lake. Eventually my parents moved there when I was at Riverdale. Cayuga College, where I began to teach, was also nearby. The college reminded me of the small colleges in New England with a beautiful landscaped quad in the middle. On each side were red brick buildings with huge white columns. Marianne taught at Hobart and William Smith Colleges in Geneva, New York. However, that didn't last long because she became pregnant with Sara as soon as we were married, and then it wasn't long before we had Jake.

After we lived in Skaneateles for about seven years, things sort of got complicated, as I explained earlier. Marianne seemed to be in a funk all the time. She had her running and her sometimes crafting with the beads, and she, like me, got tired of the people we went out with and their superficial posturing. But eventually she accepted them.

– – –

It was getting dark and the search on Route 20 turned up nothing. The older ladies including that Darlene lady were gone, so I started to walk back toward Bill and Rose's house. Just then I received a call from Neil, at the college, and he said that the president called again and was upset about another article I wrote. This one was entitled "Higher Education's Caste System." He told Neil it was bullshit like the other one. I thought about that for a moment and how wrong he was, again. In fact, some parts of my article were quoted by a *New York Times* writer who was writing on inequality in higher education. What the fuck is going on? It's another article I wrote several years ago. Why is the president now so interested in me and my articles I wrote years ago?

Most of all, like before, the president complained that I was always writing about education rather than English or literature—but you see, no one reads the obscure English journals that talk about phenomenological meanings, postmodernism, feminist theories, and deconstruction of the aesthetic and the hermeneutics of life, and so on, and so on. Who cares about these issues? I thought people in higher ed and the public do care about issues they face in their daily lives such as the caste system. If we look back through the history of higher education, it is quite evident that we have a well-defined caste system with certain schools at the top of the heap and others at the bottom. Prestige may or may not play a major role in establishing the public perspective, but for the most part it does.

## Looking for Marianne

The scholar Isabel Wilkerson offers a transformative framework in order to understand the caste system. The social hierarchy that begins categorizing people by birth especially leads to injustices. She goes on to say, "... the hierarchy of caste is not about feelings or morality. It is about power—which groups have it and which do not." All of this fits the higher education system even more so today.

– – –

It was nice to be with Jake and Sara last night after the Route 20 search. We drove into Auburn and ate at the Sunset Restaurant. Marianne and I discovered it about a couple years ago. The food was good, and the atmosphere was made up of neighbors in the area. The dark paneling reminded me of something out of the seventies. The bar was huge and circular. Everything about it was cozy and home-like. Nothing like the cookie-cutter restaurants of today.

Both Jake and Sara kept asking throughout dinner when Marianne was coming home.

Sara asked, "Why did she leave?"

"She had to take care of some business," I said. "You know how she likes to make things out of beads?"

"Yes," said Sara. "I just want her home, and I think it's something more."

"You may be right," I said. "I don't know anymore."

"Why are so many people coming to Grandpa and Grandma's? Are they looking for her too?"

"They are, but it's okay. She'll be back in a few days. So, don't worry."

"I'm really worried, Dad," Jake said, almost crying.

"Look, don't worry," I said. "She'll be back. I miss her too."

Then I changed the subject and I asked them about school. Stubbornly, they still kept asking about Marianne and when she was coming home. They were persistent but eventually I think believed me that Marianne was coming home.

After we finished dinner, I drove them to Bill and Rose's. They seemed in better spirits by the time I left them off.

I decided afterwards to call Abby.

"I wish I could come over. I miss you," I said.

"I miss you too," she said. "Oh, that Holly girl called again and wants to meet face to face and talk to me about your taking advantage of me because I'm a vet. You look for vulnerable girls, she said, and then groom them for your sex toys. I told her I'm my own person and nobody is controlling me."

"Good," I said, "She just wants to get in on the 'Me Too' movement. I knew she would be trouble when I met her."

"Paul, let's forget her."

"Okay, I know the police are watching every move I make, so it's hard to get over to see you."

"I know, because every once in a while, they drive by here."

"Shit, we'll have to wait this through." I said, "Somehow we'll get together, understand?"

"Yes, I do. I just wish all this Marianne stuff was over with."

"So do I, hon. Take care, love you."

"Love you too," she said.

As I now parked, down the street from my house, there was a ping and text from Marianne. Fucking media trucks were all over.

*Pretty soon you and that whore will be free of me. I think I know who it is. We met her at the Blue Goose and you introduced me to her as one of your senior students. I saw how all hot and flustered you got. You introduced her as Abby, a vet who was finishing her degree. Deep down, I could see that there was something between you two. But I don't care anymore. I'm planning to end this soon. I just wish I could sleep at night though. Another thing, it seems like all we have done these last few years is argue: about the kids, about money, about my not taking showers and how much I stink. Of course, you're perfect. I hated it, how you were always scratching your balls and breathing on me at night with garbage breath. I just don't want to be alive anymore.*

– – –

Early the next morning I was awakened by a steady pounding on the front door. I threw on my sweats and went down and opened the door. *Fuck*, I thought, *it's the police, Harrison and Kohl.*

Kohl asked, looking all serious, "Can we come in?"

"Sure," I lied. *You're already fucking in*, I thought.

They quickly came in and sat on the sofa as I sat across from them.

"First of all, Paul, how are you doing?"

"Okay, I guess."

"Well," Harrison said, "I want to know if your wife had any affairs? Or do you know if she had a crazy boyfriend when she was younger?"

"She did talk about a guy named Red who she went out with in high school and who had a terrible temper."

"Where did she go to high school?"

"Pebble Hill, a private school in Syracuse."

"You don't know of anyone around here stalking her or threatening her?"

"No, everyone loved her."

"Well, look," Kohl said in a tone like I think we're onto something, "if you think of anyone who was mean to her, give us a call."

"Sure." *Assholes*, I thought.

After they left I took a shower and I thought about Abby and how much I really loved her. It is so wonderful being in love. You always want to be with that person and carry that person with you. It seems you can't function without seeing or hearing from that person. You want that person to be with you every minute of the day. I know it sounds corny, but that's what I think the meaning of love is. *Still, however,* I thought, *pretty young girls turn me on.*

A wave of depression later came over me. *What Marianne has is contagious,* I thought. *And who is the person she mentioned in that text that loves her?*

– – –

That night, as I sat in the kitchen drinking a large glass of wine, I heard a soft knocking on the back door. Through the window I could see it was Abby. Quickly, I opened the door.

"How the hell did you get here?"

"I walked the backyards. I had to see you." She then threw her arms around me and gave me a hard, hot and open kiss.

"Did you see any police?" I asked anxiously while I broke the kiss.

"No," she said, aggressively pushing me into the dark living room. She then took my hands and placed them on her hard breasts.

"I want you to touch me all over, please. I want you."

I didn't want to because I was worried about the police showing up, but I did make love to her anyway, and afterward Abby cuddled in my arms and looked up at me with her face and eyes glowing.

"I love you so much," she said.

"So do I. I never loved anyone like you before, but Abby, I told you we have to be careful because the media attention is getting out of hand. You gotta go. I wish you could stay, and maybe someday it will be all different. Please," I pleaded.

I notice from the living room that dawn was breaking and the lake across the street seemed to be on fire.

Finally, she got up, dressed, pecked me on the cheek, and left out the back door.

– – –

With the media following me, I drove over to Bill and Rose's home. It had been almost two weeks that Marianne has been gone. Getting out of the car, Snake came rushing up to me and announced, "Look, last night I went over to Columbus Street in Auburn. They have some good weed and pills of any kind. Anyway, this one creepy-looking guy said he saw Marianne's picture in the paper and thought Marianne used to come over every few weeks looking for drugs. Someone told him that you and I were friends. I think we should go over tonight when all the freaks come out. I'll see if some of my friends can come too. What do you say?"

"Sounds good."

"We'll meet here around eleven tonight, okay?"

"Okay." I thought, as I now approached the table with the coffee and doughnuts, what the hell was she doing over there? She could have been raped or killed. *Jesus, Marianne, what other life did you live?*

– – –

**Looking for Marianne**

One weekend when we were visiting my parents, Freddy, I could see they were at a point in their lives where they hardly spoke to each other. Much of their time was spent sitting in front of TV watching old *I Love Lucy* episodes, and as we were preparing to leave this one time, I noticed my father was still in the den napping. My mother directed me to go wake him and tell him we were leaving. I went in the den and tried waking and helping him up. He opened his eyes and mumbled something I didn't understand. I tried lifting him up. He couldn't get up. All of his body parts seemed paralyzed.

"Help!" I yelled out to Marianne and my mother. "Call the EMS. He can't move."

My mother rushed in and tried moving him by pinching his arm. Nothing happened.

"Jimmy, get up," she cried out angrily. "Paulie is going. Get up."

He mumbled, "Just let me be."

Soon the EMS was there and placing him on a stretcher. One of the EMS people, who looked about fifteen, asked him, "What's your name, buddy?"

A weird voice responded, "Jim."

They then wheeled him down the hall while my mother screamed in the background, "Paulie, make sure you get his wallet out of his pocket."

One older paramedic had it in his hand and gave it to me while smiling like he understood. My mother trusted no one. On the way to the hospital, I rode up front with the driver who seemed to be a huge lumberjack type with a thick, red beard and tender-looking blue eyes. All we talked about was his schedule and how tired he was. Nothing was said about my father in the back. Death or an upcoming death were not topics for small talk.

Once we were in the hospital, a nurse cut off my father's pants and put him on a ventilator. Soon a middle-aged doctor came in and said he thinks that my father had a TIA. He went on to say the CAT scan and other tests would confirm his diagnosis. Probably, he said, he had many more TIAs in the past and now the blood was finding it more difficult to get through the narrowing arteries to the brain.

A nurse with a blue streak running through her black hair was standing by the doctor and said, "There's not much we could do for your dad except insert a feeding tube in his stomach. That'll maybe give him twenty or thirty more days."

"To live?" I asked.

"Yes, I'm sorry to say," she said. I noticed now her gold tongue ring showed as she talked. She had a wide, seductive smile. *Shit, I can't think of her tongue ring now. My dad is dying now. Please, God, help me.*

"When he's fully conscious I'll ask him about the tube." *Forget the nurse, Paul, forget her.*

That night I sat with my father for hours before he became fully conscious. Death was moving in quickly. His eyes seemed empty in their sockets.

"Dad, do you want them to insert a feeding tube in your stomach?"

With a halting weak voice, he responded, "No. I can't walk anymore, or hardly talk, and food drips out of my mouth like this morning when they were trying to feed me. You saw it. I'm already half dead. Let me go, Paulie, I have nothing to live for. Your mother is a bitch. I should have left her years ago. Please let me go." He died ten hours later.

When I called my mother and told her that he was dead, she showed no emotion. With bitterness in her voice, she said, "Let's see how many of his women show up at the funeral. I'm not going, just tell them I'm sick. And, Paulie, I want you today to get rid of all his clothes. He can't hurt me anymore."

I thought back to what my father said before I left to go to his hospital bathroom. "You know Oprah knows the script for this country. She knows how we'll die."

"Dad," I asked, "What do you mean?" I thought, *Why is he talking about Oprah?*

Those were the last words he ever spoke to me. Another thing I noticed as he laid in bed, the huge fingers he had, and I thought how many women's breasts he had cupped with them.

Even though I knew he managed the Talman's grocery chain, I knew very little about the details of his past life. I had to make up almost all the obituary. The school and year of his college graduation were all made up.

And on top of all this, I couldn't get over my father's clothes as I threw them into garbage bags for the Salvation Army. He owned about thirty suits and several sportscoats. He was a sharp dresser. I always thought that he looked like the actor David Niven. He was tall, thin, and strong. The neatly trimmed mustache made his strong facial features stand out. Marianne often said I took after him because I always dressed with the finest of polo shirts, V-necks, and tailored pants.

My dad loved bow ties. I think I counted over two hundred as I threw them in the garbage bags. On the other hand, I had only a few ties because of the casualness of today's professors. Most of my father's clothes were tailored at Leabury's in Syracuse. They no longer exist. He also had several pairs of shoes that were still in the original boxes unopened.

My mother's clothes were also very expensive. She bought them from Edwards and Deys department stores in Syracuse. They are also long gone. However, she wears almost the same clothes almost every day now. Because she's always cold these days, she wears a thick multi-colored sweater made up of reds, greens, blues, purples, and some black and white here and there. Underneath, she wears a very thick black turtleneck with black pants. The shoes she wears now are expensive nurse's sneakers.

Often I think, *Why I didn't know them better?* He was distant and she was cold, and she hated to be touched or hugged. A funny thing about my father, I thought, deep down he really loved me but couldn't express it. The only time, as I said earlier, I saw any emotion from him for me was around when I left to go back to Riverdale or Harvard.

— — —

## Looking for Marianne

Marianne had been missing almost a month now,
*First—*
*A few days passed.*
*Then a week.*
*Then two.*
*Now a month.*
So one afternoon, I took the kids after school to a play area at Destiny Mall in Syracuse. It's one of the largest malls of its kind with over 250 places to shop. I liked bringing the kids to the amusement part of the mall. They loved the racing cars. We did that for a good while and then afterwards we went to dinner at the Cheesecake Factory. Throughout dinner they kept asking about Marianne again.

"Have you heard from Mom?" Sara asked.

"Not yet," I lied.

Later, walking out of the mall, and holding their hands, they cried a little.

– – –

As we planned, I met Snake at the volunteer center in front of Bill and Rose's house. There were now huge spotlights shining on the area. Snake was standing with three overweight guys who looked like they were great high school athletes at one time but now in middle age, they had let their bodies go because of too much eating and drinking. He introduced me to them: Pudgy, Frankie, and Sweets. Wonderful, I thought. Mafia thugs from the area. Jesus.

Snake said, and nodding in their direction, "I thought we may need them in case something comes up."

"Okay," I said.

We drove to Columbus Street in Snake's Mercedes. Columbus Street ran parallel to an old locomotive factory called ALCO, which at one time in Auburn employed over one thousand workers. Across from the factory, I noticed a lot of empty stores and restaurants but also a few bars and fast-food places that were still open. The area was dominated by Blacks and Hispanics. Most of the whites had moved out to the middle-class areas of Auburn. As throughout America, the rich were winning and the poor were losing. The caste system is firmly in place.

Snake led the way to a bar called Smokey's. Once inside, I knew why it was called Smokey's. It was full of thick, blue smoke and you could hardly see anyone. All you could make out were sweaty bodies dancing to loud rock music with a female singer yelling "Love sucks, love sucks." The guys looked zonked out on pills and alcohol. The women, or should I say girls, all looked underage. They hardly wore anything except string-like halter tops and miniskirts with no underwear underneath. Snake left for a few moments and then brought over a guy who was dressed in a tight white shirt and black pants that seemed pressed into his legs. He had black, shoulder-length hair with an unkempt grayish beard. I thought he looked like a young Jeffrey Epstein.

"Paul, this is Phil, who just told me that Marianne was here a few weeks ago."

"Hi," I said as I shook his hand lightly. Whatever diseases he had, I didn't want.

"I'll tell you, buddy, after Snake described her, I remembered her. She was hot stuff."

"Thanks, but how many times has she been around?"

"I don't know," he said. "She would come in, buy a drink, and buy some Fentanyl and Oxycontin from me. I think she would get a month's supply and come back again in a month or so. I noticed sometimes she would dance a couple times, then leave."

"Please call Snake if she comes in again," I said as serious as I could.

"Got it, man," he said.

Soon afterwards, we left and went to another bar down the street called "Bald Eagle." It seemed a lot more subdued and classier. Some of the guys were even wearing suits, while most of the women were in tight flashy gold or silver dresses. Guys were dancing with guys and women were dancing with women.

Snake said, "Gays and lesbians hang out here, with some straights."

He called a woman over with huge breasts and purple hair.

"Shelly, this is my friend Paul, his wife is missing. She's a classy-looking woman who might have come by looking for opioids or stuff like that."

"You got a picture of her?" she asked. Nodding to me, she said, "I've seen you on TV."

## Looking for Marianne

"Right," I said as I pulled a photo out of my wallet and showed her a picture of Marianne. She stared at the picture for a long time.

"Yeah, I've seen her. A nice person. She got hooked up with a young girl named Rebecca. But I haven't seen her or Rebecca in a few months. The young ones come and go, especially if they hook up. You know what I mean? I hope you find your wife," she said. "It's sad."

"Shelly, give me a call if she comes in again," I said. I handed her one of my cards from the college with my name and phone number on it.

I thought, *What the hell would Marianne be doing here?*

As we headed back to the car, we saw two hulks trying to break into Snake's Mercedes Benz. Suddenly Snake's friends ran ahead and shoved them away. Snake's friend Pudgy really did a number with the butt of his pistol on one of the guys. Then we jumped into the car and sped away. I saw blood dripping on the windshield of the car.

When we got back to Bill and Rose's place, it was desolate except for a few camera crews. As I was thanking Snake and his friends I got a call from Abby.

I moved away and answered. "Look," I whispered in the phone, "I love you too."

She was crying, "Paul, I need to see you every day. I just need to know you still love me. I'm coming over."

Snake heard everything from standing in the rear of me, and now, full of anger, said, "What the fuck was that? Are you fucking someone while Marianne is missing? You're crazy." He threw up his hands in disgust.

"It's a long story," I said. "When we get more time, I'll explain it to you."

"You know there's already talk on the street about you killing Marianne."

"I know."

As I started walking toward my car, I heard him say, "I hope to hell you know what the fuck you're doing, buddy."

Freddy, I should have told you about the whole Columbus Street thing. I'm sorry.

That night, Freddy, I thought about what the poet Peter Franklin wrote:

> *I don't know how much*
> *Longer I can be a fraud.*
> *Saying things I don't mean*
> *And know as soon as I*
> *Say it that I'm lying.*
> *Is there anything that I say*
> *That I do mean, or is*
> *It all a lie?*

— — —

It had been *forty-four* days now that Marianne had been missing. Earlier in the day, Rose had called. She was upset because she thought the police were doing nothing. I agreed with her as she hung up.

I waited by the back door with only a large moon shining in. I didn't want anyone to know I was home. The whole Columbus Street experience was still upsetting. And I also knew Abby would be there soon.

As I saw Abby bringing her hand up to knock, I quickly opened it and grabbed her hand and pulled her in. Like a starved animal, she was all over me as she pushed me into the living room. And almost too aggressively, I pushed her away.

"Abby, I love you very much, but we have to stop this until things settle down."

"I know, but I can't live without you."

"Well, we have to cool it for a while."

"What should I do while I'm waiting to see you?" she sobbed.

"Study and get ready for your semester finals. My Lit exams are going to be tough."

"Okay, but will you at least call me every day and tell me that you love me?"

"Yes," I lied.

After she left I took a long hot shower, which helped with the stress I was feeling.

Early in the morning I got another text from Marianne:

> *I got to tell you that saying yes is easier than saying no is the moral of the story. I want you to know, especially these past few years, our sexual encounters gave me no physical or emotional*

*pleasure. I wanted to appear I was pleasing you, but I never felt anything. I think you know that. I was faking it, like you. You see I think you enjoyed sex more in your head. You go to that place and it's more real to you and more enjoyable than anywhere else. We have been faking it for years, except for the first years of our marriage. Even my orgasms were fake. "Oh Paul, stop, stop ..." Does that sound familiar? Everything is so dark today in my spirit. I want it to end and nothing I want to accomplish seems attainable. You know, Paul, we are both dark people. The next text may be my final.*

– – –

Freddy, I remember, I was terribly upset that you didn't attack the prosecution when they used Marianne's texts. The prosecution said that the texts proved that we were having major problems. I didn't like it when they shared her thoughts about our private sexual life. I murdered her, they said, because Marianne was unable to satisfy me. That's bullshit. Marianne was mentally ill. I mean a few months before all this happened, I would be talking to her about something, and then she would suddenly stop and start talking about something else. On and on it would go. I couldn't carry on a conversation with her. She was all over the place. She couldn't concentrate on anything except her depression and how I was destroying her life.

— — —

The next day, which was now the forty-fifth day Marianne was missing, I was driving back to the college to teach and also to keep an appointment with the president. Neil said that he's pretty upset about yet another article I wrote, which appeared in the *Harvard Journal*. "The president said it was a bunch of crap about chaos theory and teaching. The president said, 'I know crap when I see it, and why is he still writing this shit and not literature things like I told him, like examining Dickens and his writing.'" That article the president was talking about I wrote five years ago.

Freddy, I know you're probably bored with this stuff but I got to get this out. Anyone who has done any teaching knows that no formula, no rule, no theory ever works perfectly with the students. The teaching we have today seems to be creating passive, unresponsive, non-thinking, dependent students.

But a new view of teaching comes from the study of chaos theory. As I wrote, the theory says that elaborately complex systems are unpredictable. A person leaves the house thirty seconds late, escapes a falling flower pot by millimeters, and then is run over by a truck. Thus, small variables in one's daily life can have major consequences later on.

We can see good teachers working on their artistry as they attend to the chaotic nature of the classroom moment by moment. Good teachers are like jazz musicians. They respond and improvise to the critical points in their music as they play implicitly or explicitly, and they recognize there is order in the disorder of their worlds.

— — —

The president's office was in a gray stone building that looked medieval, and his office was in a small tower on the top of the building, typical of a castle.

As President Ames's secretary brought me to meet him in his office, he looked to me like an overweight salesman. He was short, balding, and barrel-chested. He sat behind a huge brownish mahogany desk. He stood up, shook my hand weakly, and motioned for me to sit in a gray straight-back chair in front of his desk.

"First of all, Dr. Testa," he said smiling, "I know your students love you."

"Thanks." I thought, *Cut the bullshit mister gladhander, and let's get to why I'm here.*

"To be honest with you, Paul, what's with these articles you're writing? They have nothing to do with English," he looked down and I could see a copy of my article on chaos theory on his desk, with all sorts of red markings on the words and in the margins. He had circled many words, including: Bifurcating, Dysfunctional, Attractors, and Dynamic quality.

"Do you want me to explain each of those terms to you? Some of those articles I wrote a long time ago. Again, I can explain the terms."

"That's not necessary," he said in a very serious tone. "Paul, you don't belong here at Cayuga. You belong at Harvard or a place like that, not here."

"What are you saying?" I asked with my chest tightening and my face burning.

"You don't have tenure and you've been an associate for many years. I just think it's time for you to move on. I know you have that problem with your wife missing, but finish this fall semester, then you gotta go."

"Are you saying I'm fired?"

"I guess I am. You're too smart for us, Paul."

"Is it because of the articles?"

"Basically, yes. I mean, we also did have a complaint from a girl student that felt you touched her inappropriately."

"What are you talking about?" I asked, shaking inside.

"Listen carefully, Dr. Testa," he said angrily now, and with a beet-red face. "If you fight this, by saying censorship and all that shit, we will bring up the touching incident."

"Look, President Ames," I said sucking up to him, "I've been voted outstanding teacher for two years in a row."

"I know," he said, patronizing me.

"I mean students have said on their evaluation comments that I have changed their lives—"

"I know, I know," he interrupted me. "But we can't have professors touching students inappropriately, that's what the policy says. Oh. I also heard that there's talk about you and another student having an affair. I hope that's not true, because if it is, you got a problem, fellow. Now I got to go to another meeting. I think it's best that you leave. That's it."

He suddenly stood up and left while I sat there, somewhat down-beaten by his comments. Then I thought about how much I loved teaching. There was nothing like seeing students get turned on when I explained the complexity of James Joyce's writing and how that connects with the modern-day writer Joyce Carol Oates. Eventually I was able to show them how both writers connect with Homer's *Odyssey*. Teaching, I thought, was the only thing stable in my life right now.

I can't remember, Freddy, driving home that afternoon, I was so worked up. The firing, the inappropriate touching thing. The president was no different than many higher ed administrators. They lie. Welcome to the liars club, Mr. President. They also hate conflicts or confrontations so they weasel around the real issues. That's what the president did pretending that my articles were the problem, when it was really about touching a student inappropriately. I wondered who it was. That high school girl Holly or her parents came to him. I don't know. See, Freddy, I touch students all the time to show that I care about them. Perhaps I've gone too far with some. Anyway, my life was coming apart.

### Looking for Marianne

When I got home and walked to the front door, the media's questions being asked faded into the background because of the dazed and shaken state I was in. However, it didn't last for long. I got a text from Harrison saying he and Kohl would be there the next day at ten in the morning. There were some more things that needed to be cleaned up. I thought now of a short poem from Peter Franklin I had students read:

*Man is like a burning*
*Candle.*
*The inner is burning*
*And dissolving and spilling*
*Over to the outside*
*But eventually it burns out*
*Man keeps getting closer*
*And closer to the order*
*Of things but*
*Death is the only*
*Time inside and outside*
*Become one*
*Death is his only answer.*

Then I got this text from Marianne. *Fuck.*

*Guess what, and as you can see, I'm still alive. ... I really miss the kids. I now realize how much I missed them after being gone for several weeks. I love them so much. Last night I took something that really helped. My depression was gone for a little while. And I felt good. There was no suffering or thoughts of suicide. But, the good feeling didn't last very long. I guess I felt good for about an hour. God, if I could feel like that all day, it would be great. But now I'm feeling confused and feel really tired. I can't concentrate on anything. My body and mind don't feel right. Oh, I started running again, hoping it would help with the depression. It hasn't. But I like running now. I hope someday to run the Boston Marathon if I'm alive. How's your love life? I see you on TV every once in a while with search parties. So they're still looking for me. I hope the police are getting close to why I'm missing ...*

– – –

Freddy, let me now tell you about that girl Holly. I met her at the fitness center. It was early in the morning and very few people were there. Anyway, I was walking to the center's storage closet to get more weights and I saw this cute pony-tailed blonde follow me in. *I really like blondes.*

"Can I help?" she said.

"Sure," I said, while picking up some fifty-pound weights. My hand slid over hers as she began picking up the weights. I think my knee also pressed against her bare thighs.

"My name is Holly Adams. What is yours?"

"Paul Testa." I pressed harder against her thighs. "How old are you?"

"Fifteen," she said. "I'm a sophomore at Skaneateles Central."

I moved my hand up to her breasts thinking all along how today girls were much more mature, physically and intellectually.

Then suddenly she slapped my hand away. "Don't do that." She turned and ran out.

– – –

Harrison and Kohl showed up at eleven instead of ten. Harrison still dressed with a shirt and tie. He had no sport coat. Maybe he wanted to be my friend today. Kohl seemed to be more relaxed with a blue polo shirt and windbreaker.

Harrison spoke first. "Can we sit down?"

"Sure."

They both headed to the sofa and I took my usual place in the wingback chair across from them.

"The point is this, Paul." Kohl was really trying to be friendly, but it was all fake. "The thing is this, tell us where you were the night she went missing."

"I was right here," I lied.

"What did she say to you before she left?" he asked.

"She said she was going to drop the kids off at her parents and then drive over to the fitness center and run on the treadmill for about ten miles. She was getting ready to do a 25K in Washington, DC. I guess it's sponsored by the Marine Corps."

"Tell us, Paul, about her depression," Harrison now said.

"When we first got married she didn't have it. It seemed to come on after the kids were born."

"Is she working with some doctor?" Harrison asked matter-of-factly. "And if she is, can you tell us his or her name?"

"There is someone, I met her a couple of times. Her name is Dr. MacRoy. Really nice. I think Marianne has been going to her for a long time. I went with her a couple of times and Dr. MacRoy asked what my perceptions were about Marianne's depression."

"Do you think Dr. MacRoy would mind if we called her?" Kohl asked smiling. "Thanks also, Paul, for being honest, giving us her name. We really want to help."

"I don't know. I don't think Dr. MacRoy would mind you calling."

"Good, now we touched on this before," Harrison said. "You know most married guys every once in a while cheat on their wives. So do wives." He forced a giggle. "So, Paul, come on, have you been getting something on the side?"

"A couple years ago I got close to cheating at a conference for English teachers. You see I met this pretty brunette teacher from Southern California. But I couldn't go through with it. We just kissed a couple of times."

"You sure?" Harrison asked suspiciously.

"I'm sure. Come on guys, they're having another search party in a little while. I have to get there."

I stood up and then both detectives stood.

"Look, Paul, if we wanted to give you a lie detector test," Kohl asked in a serious tone, "would you do it?"

"I don't know. Then I'll have to get a lawyer, right? I think we're doing okay without one, don't you think, guys?" Right then and there I knew I needed a lawyer.

"Yes," they both said. "Look, Paul, we're just doing our job. You understand. And also, Marianne's parents are on us 24/7."

"They are very needy people, I know."

"Tell us," they both laughed going out the door.

— — —

When I arrived at Rose and Bill's house, I saw a group of volunteers who were going to Lake Owasco in Auburn. Someone said they thought they saw Marianne running around the lake. So I got into a blue SUV with three older women who looked like they all had had Botox treatments, as their faces looked all red and bloated.

During the ride over to Owasco, they pretended to be supportive but were more interested in flirting with me. Once we stopped at the State Park on Owasco, the women went north on Owasco road and I went south. We decided to meet back at the park in two hours. I walked slowly around some homes that looked exactly like some of the rich homes in Skaneateles.

My thoughts were on the cops' stupid-ass questions and the president's accusations. I really didn't know what student he was talking about because it's in my nature to touch students when I talk to them. In the final analysis, I got to find myself a lawyer.

When we got back, everyone was disappointed that they found nothing. So on the way back to Skaneateles, we stopped at Green Acres, one of the oldest drive-in restaurants in America. We all ate their famous hot dogs and talked about nothing really. The one woman sitting in the back with me kept touching my arm and leg as she talked about how her husband's business with investing money was doing well. I just wished she would stop touching my leg. I guess some students don't expect to be touched either.

Later, as I was getting out of the car, the woman who kept touching my leg asked me to come by. She said her husband was away on business. I told her I couldn't. I had to teach tomorrow morning and I needed to prepare.

– – –

Before I went home, I decided to stop by the Sherwood, get a drink, and see if that beauty Sandra Brown in the white turtleneck was there. As I walked in, I saw only three or four guys—sitting at the bar talking about Trump and the stock market. She wasn't there, so I grabbed a quick drink of white wine and left. When I got home, I noticed the house was completely dark. I was surprised, for usually I leave on the kitchen light over the sink. Maybe I forgot to turn it on, I thought.

Once I opened the door, I could hear muffled crying coming from the back bedroom on the first floor. I went directly to the bedroom, and there on the bed was Abby in the fetal position crying hard. I hurried to the bed and sat on the edge and began rubbing her back. She cried even more.

"What's wrong?" I asked with deep concern.

"I'm pregnant," she sobbed. "I've known for a week, but with all this stuff with Marianne, I didn't want to say anything."

"Oh my God," I said trying to be understanding as I continued to rub her back.

"I'm so sorry, Paul."

"That's okay," I lied.

"How many weeks are you?"

"About eight?" she said weakly. "I haven't been taking the pill."

"Do you think with everything going on, you should think about an abortion?" I asked.

"I don't know, it's our baby, Paul"

"I know."

"My mother's a strict Catholic. I told her not to say anything because of what's going on with you and Marianne missing. It would be awful if this got to the media."

*Oh fuck,* I thought, *what will happen if the police find out?* I picked up a green and white afghan at the end of the bed and put it over her. I kept rubbing her back and soon she fell asleep. I got up, went to the kitchen and poured myself a glass of white wine and then sat at the table and gazed into the dark. *I'm drinking too much. I gotta stop.*

I thought now I must convince Abby to have an abortion. We could go to Syracuse and have it done. I feel bad because it's my child too. I don't know, perhaps we can go to Italy and have the baby there. I've always wanted to go to Italy and see where my grandparents came from. I know it's a small village near Naples.

This is so crazy. I thought I could admit to the police I've been having an affair for almost a year with Abby. What can they do, throw me in jail for having an affair? I read somewhere close to seventy percent of today's husbands cheat on their wives. Perhaps Harrison or Kohl have done the same thing. But, Abby is my student, and that could be a problem, especially if other students come forward. After I finished the wine I went and laid down next to Abby.

The next morning, I smelled bacon frying. Abby was gone from the bed, so I got up, dressed, and went to the kitchen.

Abby was wearing one of my oxford button-down blue shirts. She looked lovely, with half of the buttons in front unbuttoned. Her figure was perfect, not like Marianne, who, as I said before, put on a lot of weight this past year.

"How about some breakfast, honey," she said tenderly.

"Sounds good," I said.

"You see, Paul, this is what it would be like if we were together." She handed me a dish of scrambled eggs and bacon as I sat down. She now sat across from me at the granite counter.

"Yes, it would be great, Abby, but we got to do something about the baby."

"What," she said, almost crying, again.

"I don't know. I'd have to think on this. You go back home, and I'll call you later, okay?"

"Okay," she said with a sorrowful look on her face. "You'll call, Paul, right?"

"I promise I will."

"Also Paul, you know I wouldn't tell anyone at school about us. I mean my mother knows about the baby but she wouldn't say anything."

"I know," I said, not really believing her. "I think we need to back off for a while, and for real now, you know. We need to spend less time in my office, the fitness center, and here in my home. You know what I mean. At least until we figure out what's going on with Marianne. The optics don't look good."

"I understand, but I'll hate it. You have my soul, now, Paul. There is no way I can live without you."

"I know," I said.

"Oh, I forgot to tell you that Holly called again and wants to really meet. She said you're charismatic and I need to watch out. Anyway, I told her to leave me alone because I love you."

"Good," I said. "Like I told you before, I knew when I first met her she would be trouble."

"Right," she agreed.

– – –

**Freddy, now, below, in this babbling letter to you I will include you and how we met. You could also see how I perceived you and the job you did. I mean, everyone wants feedback on how well they're doing. Jesus, Freddy, feedback is one of those jargon terms we use in higher ed. You think I'm going to feed a horse. Lastly, remember I'm a writer. My story and what happened to Marianne could be one of my best novels.**

– – –

Freddy, remember we met because I had heard that you were one of the best lawyers in the area. And after we met I liked you right off because you had a confident voice. And with your gray hair, well-conditioned body, I knew any jury would believe you. Most of all, you had a father-like quality to you. I was also impressed by your offices and the conference room we met in. The furniture was cherry and solid oak. The paintings were abstract and looked like you were an apostle of Pollock.

The first thing you did, you asked me if I loved Marianne, and I said, "I don't know."

Then I told you about Abby and her being pregnant, and I thought I loved her. But I also told you that I fooled around here and there before I met her.

"Okay," you said not at all surprised. You went on to say, meeting with the police or media, you would be there for me.

You also said you were going to get one of your private investigators to begin looking for Marianne.

— — —

Once I got home, after meeting with you, Freddy, I thought about some other things. I should've told you about Shirley Feinstein. She's been a major part of my life since elementary school.

This one time, and it was probably two weeks before Shirley got married, she met me at an amusement park and asked if I loved her. I said I wasn't sure. She said she would call off her marriage if I did. Anyway, she got married, but now and then we would meet over the years in nearby Syracuse hotels. One time she said if I would marry her, she would kill her husband and Marianne. And I never thought about it until now. At the time I didn't think she would ever do it. It was just her craziness talking.

Freddy, there's another thing I never told you about during the trial. It's about the time Marianne tried to kill me. It happened one night when I was robot-like making love to her. And just like that she snapped, jumped to her feet, grabbed one of the pillows, and covered my face as forcefully as she could. God, she was strong as I tried to push the pillow off my face. All the while she was screaming, "I can't stand your rejection time after time! Why do you pretend to like this? I hate you!" She then sat on my face with the pillow suffocating me. I almost blacked out, in fact I think I did for a few seconds as I had in the past, but finally I was able to raise my feet up and violently kicked her off the bed onto the floor. As she got up, she was crying profusely, and then apologized over and over again. I didn't care. We did not speak for weeks.

– – –

I drove over to Bill and Rose's house one morning, and as I was getting out of the car I got a call from Harrison telling me they were coming over to the house at noon on Sunday. I thought Harrison was cocky—smug, but not very bright. And also I thought, as you said, you wanted to be there when I met with the police.

So as I approached Bill and Rose, who were standing outside, I noticed that they were cold and standoffish. Rose began, "Paul, we are getting tired of all the media attention." She nodded in their direction.

"I know, so am I."

"Well, you've got to speak to them again."

"I will. I have a lawyer now. He can help. I'm also tired of being a suspect."

"You have to show more emotion," Rose said. "That's why people suspect you. I know it's just you, but you have to show more emotion when you talk to the media."

So we met with the media and stressed how much we missed Marianne. The kids and I wanted her home. We loved her. Rose cried as Bill became uncharacteristically silent. Sympathetically, he placed his arm around Rose's shoulders. I could see the media loved it.

I stood around for a few moments afterwards and noticed more search parties going out with TV cameras following. Soon I left to go home. I decided, even though it was a little early, to stop in at the Sherwood for a glass of wine. I wanted to check to see if Sandra Brown was there. I could see when I went in that she was there. She was wearing all black. She had on tight black slacks along with a tight expensive black V-neck wool sweater. A string of white pearls was hanging around her thin but beautifully shaped neck. I immediately took the empty stool next to her. She nodded as I sat down.

"You're Sandra Brown?" I asked businesslike.

"Yes," and you're Paul Testa, with the missing wife?"

"How come you're in Skaneateles?" I asked.

"My husband and I have a home here. We spend our weekends in Skaneateles, and in the summers we're also here most of the time. We're also good friends with Tom Cruise. He's at our house a lot. We also love the boutiques in the village. Our kids are usually gone, but in the summer they come to visit. Look, let's grab a table. I would love to talk to you about your situation."

"Okay," I said as we both got up and headed back to a table far away from the bar.

A waitress came over and took our order. She was drinking pinot grigio and I was drinking moscato.

She went on to say as she sat, "I thought I saw you here, a few weeks ago."

"I was. I live just up the street."

The drinks came and we began to sip on them now and then as she and I talked.

"How about doing an interview with me sometime soon?" she asked. "I know the media has not been too fair to you. You know I will give you a chance to tell your full story. It won't be with a bunch of microphones stuck in your face. Nationally, because of you and your missing wife, and of course because of all the celebrities that live here, Skaneateles is top in the news."

"I don't know." Deep down I thought it may be a good idea to get it all out. I know she'll ask me tough questions but they'll be fair. Also, the police would have to wait until Monday. I want the interview to come out before we meet with the police.

"Look, I'll do it, but I want it to come out Sunday night on *Sixty Minutes*."

"Wow, that's on short notice. Okay, I think I can get a crew in here and we'll do it live. How's that sound?"

"Good." I'll have all Saturday to prepare, I thought.

"We'll probably shoot around ten, sometime Sunday morning at my house. My husband's a doctor and he's gone for the weekend at a conference in LA."

"Sounds good."

"Then we'll meet at ten Sunday morning at my house. I live at 199 West Lake Road. You can't miss it. It's a huge two-story cedar home on the lake."

I thought I knew where it was; it was a huge mansion. Soon afterwards, she got up and shook my hand with both of hers. I knew she liked me and probably wanted me to come over before, but this interview had to be strictly professional. No fooling around before. *Paul, this is serious shit,* I thought.

On the way home, Freddy, I called you and told you about the interview with Sandra Brown.

"That's good," you said. "Let's get the whole story out about Abby also. I don't think we should say anything about her being pregnant now. We'll save that for some other time. I'll see you at about eight Saturday morning at your place. I'll bring Tess, my assistant; she'll help us get ready for the interview. *Sixty Minutes* is big, my friend."

"Look, Freddy, will you call the police and tell them I can't meet until Monday afternoon?"

"Sure," you said.

I hung up as I approached the front door to my house. The reporters kept yelling out questions about Marianne. Once inside, I was hoping maybe Abby was there. She wasn't. And before I went to bed, I wondered if Brown would call to ask me over tonight. We'll see. I think she's probably attracted to cases like mine. And maybe even me.

— — —

## Looking for Marianne

**Marianne had been missing now for sixty-one days.**

– – –

Freddy, you and your assistant, Tess, were there exactly at eight. I was impressed, you were dressed in a grayish tailored suit. Your hair seemed freshly cut, layered in the back and on your ears. You reminded me of the movie star Cliff Robertson. In short, I thought you were ruggedly handsome. Tessa was short, had a silver-gray bob hair style, and looked to be all business.

As we sat at the living room table, Freddy, you began.

"Paul, first of all, I noticed the other day you always seem so sad when you speak to the media. I know that's good, but I want you to talk with Sandra in an engaging conversational tone. Let your emotions come forth if you feel like it. Sometimes you seem so passive. Just be yourself and go with your gut."

"Do I talk about Abby anytime?" I asked.

"Yes," Tess said in a surprisingly friendly voice. "You want the audience to like you and feel sorry for you. Look, people fall in love with other people all the time. That's why we have divorces."

Freddy, you agreed. "The audience must feel you still truly love Marianne but they need to also understand that the marriage was falling apart. You understand?"

"I think," I said. "I'll try my best. I'm worried how convincing I could be."

"Paul, just relax," you said. "But make sure you have some notes. However, on the other hand, tomorrow you want to seem very natural in the interview. Paul you know how to do that. You've been teaching for years and probably do that all the time."

"Right," I said, while still feeling uncomfortable about being fired. I decided not to say anything to you, at least not now. You and Tess left soon after, and I was glad because I was tired and wanted to go to bed. Perhaps I should say something about the pregnancy even though Freddy said no.

I also thought about the email I received from Shirley last night.

> *Hello Paul. I have been thinking of you a lot since we saw each other. I just saw you on TV, about your wife missing. I wish I could help. Remember, I'm only a few minutes away in Syracuse. I came back from New York just last night. Anyway, I was happy we met for a few hours several weeks ago. It meant so much to me to see you, especially with my husband dying a few months ago. I've been so lonely. His Alzheimer's also killed me too. But my love has always been there for you, ever since elementary school. And even more so after we were together in the City. All my love, Shirley.*

Freddy, I thought and mentioned earlier, I must tell you about Shirley and how I met her in New York City right after Marianne went missing. No one knew I was gone. I flew in the next day, took care of my lust, and flew out. I didn't have to worry about the kids because they were over at Marianne's parents'.

– – –

The next morning, you and Tess came by to pick me up, and we drove out to Sandra's home. I was nervous as you and Tess talked about the interview. I hardly heard a word. I just wanted to get it over with.

Before I knew it, Freddy, we were driving down a poplar tree lined road to her house, which sat back from the lake. It also sat on top of a hill with not only a cedar and brick front but also a river stone façade. As we got out of the car, I looked down and saw a dock with four or five boats. I also noticed the home had a wrap-around porch. A young woman now opened the front door as we came up the porch stairs. She introduced herself as Heather, Sandra's daughter. She said she was home for the fall break. She told us she went to Cornell and was studying law. Her long chestnut hair was twisted in braids. She had deep blue eyes like her mother.

"They're getting set up in the living room. Could I get you anything to drink—coffee, tea, water?"

"Some water would be great," I said. There was a spiral staircase and, like the rest of the house, it was all hardwood. The living room was made up of a large, dark-blue sectional sofa with smaller sofas spread throughout the room. When we entered, I saw that Sandra was talking to the camera people. When she saw us, she motioned for us to join her.

"Paul, I'll have you sit with me on the sofa. I guess this is your lawyer, Fred Scott, and his assistant, Tess. Thanks for letting me know you were coming." She nodded to you, Freddy, and you nodded back with a wide grin. You then shook hands with her as she directed you and Tess to stand behind the cameras. Freddy, I think you must remember all of this.

As I sat down, they fitted me with a mic pinned to my white shirt. I was wearing a navy-blue jacket with matching pants. Sandra already had her makeup on. She was dressed in a loose-fitting black skirt, and a white blouse with a thin blue cardigan sweater.

"Now, Paul, we're going to get started once the camera guys are ready. Relax, okay," she said, as she patted my hand gently.

For the introduction to the interview, she laid out how Marianne and I had been happily married and then she just went missing.

"Paul, I appreciate your willingness to do this interview. I know our viewers would want to know right off, do you love your wife?"

"I love her very much," I lied. "And since she's been gone, my love has grown even more."

"Paul, can you tell us about the night she went missing?"

"I will, and also I'm going to tell you perhaps why she left. You see, I was doing something stupid that night."

"What do you mean?" I can see she was totally surprised.

"I was with another woman that night," I said, choking on emotion. "It was wrong, and I'm so sorry for that, and Marianne, if you're seeing this, I want you to know I realize it was a mistake on my part. I would never do it again. I was wrong. We should've gotten help because of my wandering eye. One other thing, and we'll have to deal with it. This woman is pregnant with my baby."

"So, Paul," she asked, clearly taken aback, "how long have you known?"

"I just found out."

"What will you do?"

"I don't know. I'll do whatever Marianne wants me to do."

"Do you love this woman?"

"I do. I love them both."

"Can you tell me the name of this woman?" she asked as she inched closer.

"I can't. I would rather she come forward to tell her story. This is so hard for me," I said, holding back tears.

Sandra Brown then asked some softball questions about Marianne's parents and my children. I knew what I was saying would almost destroy Bill and Rose. But I had to do it. When we were finished, Sandra looked pleased and upset at the same time. Freddy, you and Tess rushed over and got me out of the house as quickly as possible.

## Looking for Marianne

In the car, Freddy, I remember you said, "I wish you had listened to me about the pregnancy. But it's okay, that's why you're paying me the big bucks to get you out of stuff like this. I'll also be with you when you meet with the police on Monday. I know we'll be talking before that. Just make sure, Paul, when you get calls tonight from the media you refer them to me. The TV people and newspapers will be all over this when it hits tonight."

"I know, but I had to be honest," I lied.

– – –

As I pushed my way through all the reporters and got inside my house that day, I felt relieved that the interview was over. Now I poured myself a glass of wine, sat on the sofa, stared into the light coming in from outside. I thought, I have to get my mind on something other than Marianne. Usually, Freddy, what I would do is think about women. So tonight I thought about Shirley Feinstein and how we met. Freddy, I know I told you some of this before the trial but I'm going to tell you more in this letter. She's a nutcase but was always there for me. To be honest, I've forgotten most of what I told you before the trial. I think I was in shock throughout.

See, Freddy, Shirley and I met at St. Boniface Elementary. I went to St. Boniface because of the trouble I got in at Wallace Public School in Manlius. My parents were asked to come in because I had loosened some nuts on the teachers' commode so when they flushed, instead of water going down, it shot up like a geyser. I hid across the hall behind a half-closed door and watched with glee as the women teachers, especially Mrs. McGuire came out angrily shaking her dress. I hated the teachers because they were Downton Abbey types who taught with superior arrogance. They told my parents I was doing well in school, but I was a terrible discipline problem. I wouldn't stay in my seat. I was always bothering other students. And so on and so on it went. Mrs. McGuire told my parents that I was too much to handle and suggested the Sisters of Charity at St. Boniface could probably handle me better.

So the following fall I went to St. Boniface and began fifth grade where I met Shirley. I was given a seat in back of her and as I approached my seat, Shirley's big brown eyes and wide grin warmed me all over. I knew something good would come of us. I also noticed her lemon-sized breasts underneath her school uniform white blouse. I was quiet all day, staring at the curve of her neck and the perfect short cut of her bluish-black hair. I thought I was in love, and it would last forever. But the problem I had was I was too shy to talk to her for any extent of time. As the year went on, I noticed I was much better talking to the faster girls in class. I didn't want anything to spoil my image of Shirley. She was my dream girl. Loretta and Rose were fast girls and had parties at their houses. Loretta had big breasts and she loved the boys to feel her up when we played spin the bottle, whereas Rose loved practicing

French kissing with the boys. Shirley never came to the parties and stayed aloof from Loretta and Rose at school. Her parents were Jewish, and I never found out why she was at a Catholic school and not a Jewish school.

One day, Sister Bernadine caught me writing in a little black book my father had given me. I would love writing about Shirley in there. This one day, I had written about her cute button-like nose and wide lips that were made for open kisses and her breasts that were made for easy cupping. Suddenly, Sister Bernadine came up behind me and with her weapon of choice tapped me hard on the head with a ruler and told me to stand and read what I was writing.

Reluctantly, I stood, feeling my face burning as if I had a fever of 104. I began reading, but Sister stopped me quickly when I got to Shirley's breasts. I saw the back of Shirley's neck turning dark red.

From then on and until I graduated from the eighth grade, the nuns trained me to be a master altar boy as well as a bookroom boy. I went to each class and yelled "Bookroom!" One time I yelled too loudly for one nun and I got slapped hard across the face. I very seldom attended class except to take tests. Most of the time I was at the convent with Sister Aloysius, helping her cook and tend to the garden. All of this was a way to control my hyperactivity. I missed seeing Shirley and looking at her white smooth skin, not a blemish on it. I also missed looking at her lips and the delicate shape of her ears and neck. I really thought I loved her and became thrilled when I got a Valentine card from her that said "Love You," even though I knew she sent these to all the boys. She became the Blessed Virgin to me. I also learned from Kay Castro, a plump girl, how to French kiss, massage a breast, and hump on the back steps of St. Boniface in all kinds of weather. My parents thought I was at the Community Center playing basketball, not getting excited by feeling the silk of Kay's bra. I knew Shirley was too pure to ever be involved in animalistic sexual activity.

Shirley and I lost touch after St. Boniface, as my parents sent me off to public high school for two years then to Riverdale where I learned discipline and how to study. Most importantly, my English teacher, Mr. Darling, taught me to love literature and art. He was so inspirational. He was like Robin Williams in *Dead Poets Society*. He made literature come alive for me as a human being. I was able to gain insight into my life or confirm things I already knew. I thought of Shirley often and what she was doing at Albany State where I heard she was going to college then. I also heard she was going out with as many boys as she could. I wondered if she was still a virgin. I wasn't. I lost it to Lisa Epstein on her sofa. Because her parents wouldn't let her date non-Jewish boys, my name for her father was Marshal Steinberg. I did hear Shirley was serious with one guy named Jack Kelly who was tall, blond, and would pass for Troy Donahue.

At the beginning of my sophomore year at Harvard, I called Shirley out of the blue and asked if she would be my date for our Fall Festival weekend. Still, I couldn't talk to her without feeling awkward and shy.

But I knew, once we made love on this weekend she would be mine for life. Hell, I had so many girls now that I dated sometimes three on the same weekend. I had grown up to be quite handsome. I knew once she saw me and we made passionate love then I would have to beat her off me.

Alone in the car after the concert, I decided I would park in an isolated area near Wollaston Beach. Then I would kiss her, strip her naked, and give her sex she would never forget. Every single one of my friends, even though they had dates, couldn't keep their eyes off her. They looked or gazed at her as if she were some movie star. At the dance before the concert, they fought to dance with her. I didn't care because I knew what was going to happen afterwards.

Once the concert, by jazz great Dave Brubeck, was finished, we left as I had planned and drove to Wollaston Beach. I felt now that I could move on her. I placed my arm around her shoulders and pulled her closer to me as my hips pressed against the steering wheel as I tried to get her closer to my chest. I kissed her with an open mouth but her mouth remained closed. Then I tried sticking my tongue through her closed lips while my hand went for her breasts.

Suddenly she began to giggle, and then she was laughing hard; crying, she was laughing so hard.

"I've never had anyone try to neck so awkwardly. You're too funny, Paul. Let's go," she said, still laughing.

Stunned, confused, I could tell she felt nothing for me.

Wollaston Beach stood against the moonlit night and seemed to be swallowing me up whole. Sitting as close as possible to the car door, I heard her softly crying and not laughing now.

"Paulie, I'm sorry, I'm so sorry. It's not you. Something is wrong with me."

"It's okay," I lied.

– – –

The following year she showed up unannounced at Cambridge. We met at the Boston Common and there she said she loved me and apologized for laughing at me. We made love in a room at the Parker House. Surprisingly, I felt nothing and couldn't wait until she left. But I knew whenever I had lust, she would be there for me. And that's why I flew to New York after Marianne was gone for only a day.

When I got to New York, I took a taxi to where Shirley was staying. It was early afternoon in New York City. I have always loved New York because of the pulsating energy of the city. The taxi stopped in front of a classic Greco-Roman-style apartment building. As I went in, the doorman stopped me and asked where I was going. I told him about Shirley's sister living there and I was visiting. After he nodded okay, I headed up to the sixteenth floor and knocked on the door marked 16B.

## Looking for Marianne

Shirley opened the door to the apartment and I could see right away Shirley's sister had a different lifestyle. The furniture was cozy but elegant. The paintings and prints on the walls were mostly Monet and Dali. Shirley lightly kissed me as she then led me to the living room, where I looked at photos of her sister on a desktop. Her sister seemed smaller than Shirley, but more beautiful, with long sandy-brown hair and large green eyes. Shirley kept holding on to my arm as I now looked at photos of her sister with Black students in a classroom. The remaining pictures were of her sister with another woman her age holding hands, and in another one, kissing in front of the New York City Courthouse. It was signed, "Love Forever, Pam."

As we now sat on a plush sofa, I asked Shirley if her sister was gay. She said she was bisexual. Later we drank some wine. Then she offered me a joint before we made love. She also told me her sister Dianne ran a gifted program for students in Harlem. A guy from Xerox gave her sister a million dollars for the program and also another million for her. "He died last year of prostate cancer," she said. "He indulged her and loved her so much."

After making love, we decided to walk to a nearby Italian restaurant called Rex's Pasta. The afternoon sky was getting dark and dreary and it looked like rain. The blaring of the horns and thud of tires going over manhole covers matched the rapid-moving streams of people.

## Looking for Marianne

"You know," she said as we walked, "I wish I was Marianne, Paul. I'm so jealous of her. She has you and I have nobody now. As you know, my husband was sick, but also abusive, nasty, mean, and on top of that he was an alcoholic. But Paul, I'm free now." Then she began to cry. "It's so nice to have you here. I don't want to be alone again. Even though I had my husband, it was like living with a zombie."

After we ate I couldn't wait to get on the late flight back to Syracuse. My lust was satisfied and now I had to get the hell out of there. Freddy, so that's what happened when I met Shirley in New York City.

– – –

After the interview with Sandra Brown, Freddy, I decided to take a run to clear my head. I ran to Auburn and back. It's roughly about eight miles. Home again, of course I had to push through the reporters and camera people in front of the house. Once I got safely in the house without answering any questions, I was exhausted but I felt better after going through the anxiety of the interview with Sandra. I now sat down and watched the interview at seven. I thought I did a pretty good job. There were a few places I seemed a bit weak but for the most part I did okay. I came across sincere and real.

– – –

After I watched it, my phone started to blow up with calls from Abby, Bill and Rose, TV stations, and newspapers. The house seemed cold because it was the middle of fall and I had forgotten to turn the heat on. I had noticed on my run the woods turning sparse, with skeletal trees. I love this time of year when the leaves lose their yellow luster before they blow away. They always come back the next summer, with their intense colors, like civilizations that decay and then are reborn, repeated over and over again.

Ping. Now there was a text from Marianne.

*I think you need to know, you bastard, that I was going to poison you with ricin but as I saw you were not getting too sick and I couldn't add more because of our kids needed you even though I hated you. I don't think you ever understood the pain, the sadness, the loneliness, the confusion you caused me because of your philandering. I remembered this one time I followed you to Cayuga College. I saw you stop at a dorm and pick up a long-haired blonde who didn't seem any older than fifteen. Your betrayal was killing me. I was going to tell the authorities and even my parents. I wish your mother was in this world now. However, she now thinks I'm her sister. So you and that bitch are going to have a baby. What about our babies? I miss them so much. I guess you'll want a divorce. I think people need to know how you would hit me as you thrashed around in your sleep. It seemed that the only time you made love to me was when there was a flash of violence. Soon things are to be changing. You know, Paul, we only existed, and never truly lived. My sense of loneliness is really a longing for you to understand me without words. My loneliness could not be grieved or mourned. There is no getting over it. We are all lonely even though you try to forget it in the bodies of women. In a sense, loneliness will always be elusive. That's where my depression comes from. And also from you being such a cold bitch. I think you told me your mother was like that. Like mother like son.*

I turned off the phone, got in bed, and buried myself under the thick quilted covers. I wish I had been a better husband. I wondered who I was.

— — —

On Monday, Freddy, you and Tess arrived about an hour before the police were to arrive. I saw through the living room window that you had to fight through the cameras and microphones that were shoved into your faces.

Once in the house, I noticed you went to the refrigerator and grabbed a couple bottles of water, for yourself and Tess. We then sat around the dining room table. You spoke first. You said, "Paul, after we finish with the police, I'm going to make a short statement to the media. Also, I heard the police are pissed that you didn't tell them about Abby and her pregnancy."

"Too bad," Tess had said.

"Look," I said, "when I'm talking to the police, should I say something about the murder I witnessed at the private school I went to? I know I should've told you about it."

"Were you involved in it?" you asked in an understanding tone.

"Not really."

"Have the police asked you about it?"

"No."

"Then let it be. We got our hands full with this Marianne thing and now with Abby. The murder aspect is going to get louder."

"Okay," I said. "I also wonder if I should say anything to the police about Marianne, that she was trying to poison me, which I just found out in a text she sent me. And once, she tried to suffocate me with a pillow."

"Tess," you said, "get a statement from Paul about the attempted murders. We may have to use them."

"Okay," she said.

"Jesus, Paul," you said, "is that it? Anything else?"

*(Freddy, I hope I'm doing a good job now remembering our conversations before the trial.)*

"Just one other thing," I said, "I'm being let go from Cayuga College at the end of the fall semester for so-called controversial articles I have written and for supposedly touching a student inappropriately, which I never did."

"Shit. That could be a problem, especially with all the shit going down thanks to the Me Too movement. But I may be able to get the judge to not let prosecutors talk about it in the trial." Freddy, you seemed to be very confident about doing this. That's why I like you.

"Sometimes I touch people when I talk to them, but that's it," I said.

"Do you know who the student was?" you asked.

"No," I said. "I'm considered one of the best teachers in the college."

"Tess," Freddy you said, "look into it. See if you can find out who the student is. Also, Paul, I got word from a friend that Abby is going to make a statement later today. She has a hotshot woman lawyer from New York City."

"Oh shit," I remember saying, worried. "I don't know how much more I can take."

"Well, there is another thing," Freddy, you said, very seriously. "One of my investigators thinks Marianne is in Swallow Falls State Park in Oakland, Maryland. Have you and Marianne ever been there?"

"No," I replied. I remember thinking to myself when you said this that maybe I can bring Marianne home and solve our problems. We could get help and then she would accept Abby living with us and also accept the baby. I know the kids would love having a little brother or sister around. And in today's society, we have many different living arrangements, Husbands, wives, girlfriends, gay or lesbian friends, all living together.

"I want you to go there," you said, "and see if you can convince Marianne to come home with you. Do the whole thing about the kids missing her along with her parents. You know what I mean."

"I'll try," I had said.

Then there was a knock at the front door now. I got up and the police came in. Without any niceties, they immediately sat down with us at the dining-room table.

Kohl spoke first. His hair looked like it hadn't been shampooed in weeks. "Freddy and Paul, what the hell is going on? Shit, Paul, why didn't you tell us about that woman Abby and her being pregnant? I thought we were being honest with you." He was pissed.

"Look, I'm sorry," I remember you saying, Freddy, in an effective lawyer tone. "It's all about Paul not really knowing what to do and that's why I'm here to help him. And if you have any further questions I'll tell Paul what to answer and not. And from now on guys, that's it."

You remember, Freddy. Harrison and Kohl sat there stunned for a moment then Harrison spoke in a friendly voice. "Okay, I understand that's your role. But at least tell us before you people do any more interviews."

"We'll see," you said as you stood up, Freddy. "I got to get to another appointment."

"Okay," Kohl said as he also stood along with Harrison.

Freddy, remember, you led them to the front door and said, "I'm going to make a brief statement to the press about leaving Paul alone. He's dealing with a missing wife and heartbroken children who miss her. And I hate some of those fake news reports about him being a suspect."

You opened the door and let Kohl and Harrison out. We could hear the immediate screaming of questions from the media. Soon after, you left with Tess, and you both stood on my front porch as you spoke for a few moments. From the inside I could hear you say, "Please let him and his children have their privacy, and when we know more we'll let you know."

– – –

It was late that Monday afternoon when you called and said your investigator gave you more information about where Marianne was located. "She's in Cabin 1015 in Swallow Falls State Park. The cabins are near the front of the park. We also know that she runs for two or three hours on the nearby state park trails."

"Anything else?" I asked.

"Well, we know she stays in the cabin for the most part. Sometimes, the investigator said, she goes to a nearby Deep Creek resort for a meeting. The investigator thinks the person is her therapist. The sign on the outside of the house says 'Sherri Glover Counseling Services.' Oh, something else, a good-looking woman came by and stayed for a few weeks. We're getting more info on this."

When I hung up, I looked up Oakland, Maryland, on my phone and also Swallow Falls State Park. I saw the park is home to Maryland's largest free-falling waterfall along with several other smaller falls. On its website, it said there were hiking, cross-country, and skiing trails available. I also wondered who the fucking woman was that came by.

The next day, Tuesday, around four in the morning, I ran to my car, which was parked down the street. Our house, like so many others on East Genesee Street, did not have a garage. As I was opening the car door, I was shocked to see that several camera crews had followed me, along with reporters who were yelling out, "Paul, where's Marianne?" "Paul, did you kill your wife because of your love for Abby? What are you going to name the baby? ..."

Once in the car, I drove down Genesee and onto Route 41, and eventually, onto Interstate 81 South.

– – –

On the drive along Interstate 81, I had a lot of time to consider what I was going to do when I saw Marianne. Anyway, for some reason, I decided to call Shirley. I stopped and called her on my cell.

"Hi, I'm on my way to where Marianne's located."

"Where is she? I feel so bad that she is doing this to you and your kids. Thank God, Greg, my husband, and I couldn't have kids. However, I would love to see your kids someday."

"Maybe you will someday. She's at Swallow Falls State Park in Maryland, apparently."

"That would be nice," Shirley said. "Paul, I'm getting in my car now, and will be there as soon as I can. I won't stop for anything. I'm coming, I don't care what you say."

"Okay, perhaps you can help."

"I'll call when I get there."

"Sounds good."

A couple of hours later as I was driving on Interstate 70 West, I got an email from you, Freddy, with an attachment of Abby's video statement. I figured I should stop again, so I could see it. Nearing the next exit I got off and found a McDonald's, and while eating a fish sandwich, I looked at the video. It was Abby and someone who the announcer said was her lawyer standing in front of a bank of microphones, and also in the rear was that little bitch Holly Adams and an older man, who the announcer said was her father. Holly had a shitty-ass grin on her face. I also noticed Abby's lawyer was an attractive woman with long shining black hair, narrow nose, wide grin, and thick lips. She flashed a fake smile and glanced around. I thought why the fuck did Abby have a lawyer? Was it because of the *60-Minutes* interview or someone in the Me Too movement got to her?

"Abby Flatts," the announcer said, "will make a statement now. No questions will be taken."

Abby had her hair tied up in a bun. She wore a loose-fitting black dress with an opening near the neck without showing cleavage. She spoke firmly without any sobbing. "I love Paul very much, and I thought he would eventually get a divorce from his wife. But now I just hope they find her. Then things can work out. I know he loves me, and I know he'll love our child that will be coming in a few months. You see, I have had Paul for courses at Cayuga College for almost two years. We fell in love after the first year. I'm not going to call myself a victim either like some women are doing. Yes, I couldn't let go because I love him so much, and at times yes, he jerked me around and lied to me about Marianne. So I have to protect myself and our baby."

I thought now about how much I enjoyed sliding my hand up her thigh and cupping her skirt and hiking it up to her waist. We were lucky never being caught doing this in the late afternoons in my office.

Her very classy lawyer now stepped in front of the microphone and said, "That's all she's going to say until they find Marianne Testa. And if this doesn't resolve soon we'll move on the abuse front." She nodded to Holly, and smiled to her and her father.

Reporters were yelling out questions as the lawyer turned and led Abby out of what looked like a conference room.

Driving again, now on Interstate 68 I thought about Abby and the baby. I can't deal with all of that now. I've got to figure out what I'm going to do when I see Marianne. And why the fuck was Holly there? Is there an abuse charge coming?

Right then I heard a ping. I looked down and saw it was another text from Marianne, so I pulled to the side of the road and read:

## Looking for Marianne

*You know I saw your girlfriend on TV a little while ago. Asshole, you need to know something I never told you about. Plain and simple I hated raising the kids. I hated them and they hated me. There were times I wanted to smash their heads against the walls or even sometimes I thought of drowning them across the street in Skaneateles. I thought it was postpartum but it was more than that. I just hated being around them. I just wanted out. In fact the harder I tried to feel for them, the harder I felt nothing. I'm now on a journey, for once in my life having no responsibilities ... It's like when you get on a plane and your baggage has been taken care of and you're finally free. Paul, I have failed you and the kids. I know that now. I hadn't anticipated the choices and sacrifices I would have to make for our children. It was so hard to raise them and also take care of your needs. I'm a failure. I'm also a fraud like you. I'm nobody. I think everyone in this world is a fraud. Your girlfriend, my parents, and all those that are pretending to look for me. They just want attention. But make no mistake. I want to be dead. Then I would have no one to please. There's one other thing I've been thinking about. You used to say I love you to me, but if you did, it was only in an abstract and inattentive way. You treated me as one of those abstract articles you write that hardly anyone understands. And another thing. Your writing stole from us. Your writing was always first, along of course with screwing any woman that was around. I hardly existed for you. You know even though I have my friend's love, I'm no good for the kids, my parents, and even you because of the way I am now.*

After I read this, I thought Marianne is close to suicide, more than ever.

According to my GPS, I was about 100 miles away from Swallow Falls. Back on the road, I began speeding, going eighty and ninety miles per hour. An hour later, I got to Swallow Falls, went directly to the cabins out front, and just sat outside in the car. Tall hemlocks seemed to dominate the silent woods. And then suddenly as I was thinking about what I would say to Marianne I saw her, she opened the door to 1015 and began to do stretching exercises. As soon as I opened the car door, I yelled her name.

With a look of surprise she began to run to a nearby trail.

I yelled again as I ran after her, "Marianne, please, let's talk! Marianne!"

I kept running after her. We ran by huge boulders, tall trees, and finally a tall crashing waterfall as I caught up to her and wrestled her to the ground. There I sat on her and pinned her arms to the ground. I could see she was scared as I began to move off her but then all at once for some stupid reason I kissed her and she kissed me back. I touched her breasts and roughly she touched me below, and like that, with our clothes half off, she screamed, "I hate you, I hate you!" She dug her nails in my back, became rigid, and then suddenly released her hands from pressing on my back.

Hurriedly, she got up and while pulling her sweats up, screamed, "Paul, I just want to be left alone, please! What the hell is wrong with me? I don't know why I just did that with you."

She walked swiftly to the edge of the falls in front of us.

As I stood up rushing to her, I pleaded, "Marianne, I'm sorry. It was all a mistake with Abby. We can get help. We have two beautiful kids who need us."

"You're such a fucking liar," she said tearfully turning around and looking at me. And like a crazed woman, she began to violently beat me on my chest with her clenched fists. As I tried to get her to stop, I slipped on the edge of the falls, grabbing one of her legs on the way down. From that moment on, I can't remember what really happened. Fuck, Freddy, as I said to you before, I think I blacked out for a few seconds. And just like that she was gone. I came to, but everything was a blur from then on. The thunderous noise of the falls seemed to get even louder. The next thing I knew Shirley was struggling to lift me up.

"You okay?" she said as I stood up. "What happened?" she asked.

"I don't know. I was holding onto her leg, and then she was gone. I can't remember." I began to cry so hard I couldn't catch my breath. Shirley held and comforted me for a long time.

Marianne's body was found several hours later by the local rescue team. They said she died on impact. Soon after, the Oakland Police accused me of pushing her off the falls. They transferred me to Skaneateles where I was booked by Harrison and Kohl. I never saw Shirley again until this trial.

Harrison and Kohl later told me Shirley said she saw me push Marianne off the edge.

– – –

Freddy, as I had said before, I've had a lot of time to think in here. I remembered during the trial when you said the prosecution was digging up stuff about Riverdale. But I was lucky both Jim and Henry said I wasn't involved in the shooting.

As you know, Freddy, they both pleaded guilty, with no trial because they heard what happened to me. They got ten years with parole possible after five years. You know, if they were Black, they would've gotten life with no parole. There is the caste system working again. I got, if you remember, five years with parole possible after two years, added to the twenty years I got for the second-degree manslaughter for Marianne's murder. I still think that's unfair. That's why, Freddy, I want to get a new trial. Sometimes I think maybe I did push her because she wanted peace all her life. I don't know. It's so fuzzy, damn it!

Freddy, I heard also that Shirley now lives in my house, which Bill and Rose always owned. She helps with taking care of Jake and Sara. I hope to see my children someday.

You know I don't think my children were ever fooled. They knew the truth existed behind my fake smile and telling them Marianne would be back.

I know I won't see my children for some time because of how much hate Bill and Rose now have for me, and they have custody. Recently I also heard that Abby and Shirley have become good friends. Abby wrote me. You know I have a new son whose name is Paulie and plays with Jake and Sara. I'm happy for that.

Also, Freddy, I think sometimes that both Marianne and I were sociopaths. One time I caught her in a lie and yelled at her, "Don't lie to a liar." I can't even remember the lie now because I lied all the time. I read also somewhere sociopaths have little ability for remorse and empathy. That's more like me than Marianne because sometimes she was kind, thoughtful, and compassionate.

Joyce Carol Oates somewhere said that husband and wife should live affectionately like brother and sister. There would be fewer divorces, and if lust arises the couple should take care of it—or with other members of the community like the Oneida community often did. I think Marianne and I would have survived longer if we lived that way.

Also, I forgot to tell you, Freddy, about something I used sometimes with my girl students who I wanted to touch. I would tell them because I modeled I wanted them to send me photos of them and I would see if my modeling agency would like them. You see I told them a lie. I never showed the photos to the agency but it opened the door up for me to have a relationship with them. However, once I fell in love with Abby, I never used the modeling opening again.

Eventually, Freddy, I know the truth will come out and people will see that I never pushed Marianne. But Marianne is dead and someone has to pay and that someone right now is me.

*Again, I didn't kill her.* I just wish I could be sure.

The need for women is still there. But I never harassed anyone, Freddy. Jesus, they were all initiators, even that sicko Holly gave the impression she wanted it.

Best,
Paul Testa

# Looking for Marianne

March 20, 2020

Dear Freddy,

Just a short note to tell you I'm very upset that I haven't heard from you. I'm really depressed and sometimes when I think about how I've ruined people's lives, I want to die. I have people here who could help me do that! And as crazy as it may sound, I have a former student by the name of Ashley Harmon who wants to marry me. She thinks I'm sort of Rock Star. Please help! She comes almost every visiting day.

Last night, I thought maybe there is something wrong with me. And I need help or I'm going the way Marianne went. I don't want to, because I love my children so much and I want to see them again.

Depressed and Frustrated,<br>
Paul Testa

May 1, 2020

Dear Paul,

I appreciate all that you wrote. Good job. It will really help in our appeal. In fact, Tess is seeking to get it published as a book. With some work on your part it can be a best seller. And Paul, we are working feverishly on your appeal for a new trial. It takes time, but we think we can do it. One key aspect of your case is that your Miranda Rights were never read to you by the Oakland Police. We also found that the interrogation notes are missing from the Skaneateles Police. I'm sorry it has taken so long to respond.

Paul, my friend, what is most important is that we've got to get you to remember exactly what happened that day. Tess and I have found someone to help; she has excellent credentials. She's not only a therapist but also has used hypnosis in cases like this. If there is someone to uncover the events of that day, she'll do it.

Paul, it may take a while, but we'll get you out.

However, I've been notified by the president of Cayuga College that there are allegations from seven former students who have accused you of sexual abuse. It sounds like they have vivid imaginations, and I think they are emotionally unreliable. I'm working with the lawyers from the college about the dangers of accusations without due process. They, like us, want all of this to go away. Publicity would hurt the college's recruitment efforts. I don't think we can get it buried because that girl you told me about, Holly, and her father are accusing you of being a pedophile.

Another thing. Tess told me about a psychologist who lives in California. Her name is Elizabeth Loftus and she has done some groundbreaking work in memory. She has found that there is sort of a thin curtain that distorts our memory. Of course, the Me Too movement hates her for working with people like Harvey Weinstein and the Duke lacrosse players who were accused of rape. So if any more accusers come forward, we would use this woman from California. There goes my female clients. So be it ...

Finally, I do apologize for taking so long to get back to you, but believe me we have been working on your case every day, and I hope to get up to Auburn to see you next week. This abuse stuff—that really got me sidetracked for a while. I'm trying to get it settled out of court. We found a study that said 50% of the time it is the student who initiates and sends a signal they want to be more involved with the professor. The same thing goes on in the corporate world all the time.

Anyway, there are two areas we really need to hit on during the next trial. The first thing, Paul, and I don't know if it will be any help to us. It's about Marianne and her private life. We found out that there was a rumor floating around that Marianne was being abused by her father, Bill. There's no truth to that. Bill is a super nice guy, and he and Marianne had a great love as father and daughter. However, as you know, Paul, there are the texts from Marianne that indicate she was having an intense relationship with someone, and we think it was a woman named Rebecca from the Columbus Street area in Auburn.

My investigator confirmed this by talking to the State Park office. They said there was a woman who stayed with Marianne for a few weeks. They said she was young and beautiful. A woman in the office said she looked like a tall Jennifer Lopez, the singer and actress. The thing is, we have to find this woman and see if she was in some kind of relationship with Marianne. I think you mentioned in your letter to me that someone told you that Marianne was with a woman named Rebecca in the Columbus Street area of Auburn.

But I want to be honest with you, Paul. My gut says she was in a probably strong friendship with this Rebecca. I don't think it's anything more than that. I've learned from my associate, Tess, that men love to think that women who are close are always suspect of being in a lesbian relationship. Anyway, whatever relationship it was, we're not going to get much traction in a new trial from this reasoning. Unless their relationship was going sour, and then we can look into the suicide aspect.

Another area we are working on is Shirley Feinstein's strong eye-witness account, which really killed us. She seems obsessed with her love for you. We need to work on that angle more.

Cordially,<br>Freddy Scott

P.S. Your evaluation of our firm was greatly appreciated.

May 31, 2020

My Dearest Paul,
I know you must hate me because of what I said at the trial. But Paul, I had to tell the truth, my dear, even though I know you don't believe me.

Another thing, I want to tell you I know you never really loved me even though I have always loved you and probably loved you more than anyone else. You see, hon, I think once you see how well I have taken care of Jake and Sara, and your cute son, Paulie, you'll love me forever.

Every time I look at little Paulie, I see you in the biggest brown eyes I've ever seen. Like you, every girl will want him when he grows up. Like you, again, he will be charismatic and charming.

I also need to tell you that Abby is going out with the professor who took your place at Cayuga, He's middle aged, has a beard, and is a little shorter than you. He's good looking I guess. Last week she said you ruined her for life. She told me she still loves you and will forever, but you did take advantage of her and in a sense sexually abused her. I don't know. One thing I do know is that you pushed Marianne, and perhaps I helped a little by trying to pull you back. You know I always hated Marianne because I didn't think she knew how to love you.

Remember, Paul, I will always love you and I'll do anything to get you out of prison. And tell your lawyer who seems so nice that I'm willing to change some of my testimony if it will help you.

All My Love,
Shirley

Dad, I typed this letter on my tablet for me and Jake. We don't believe what some people say you did to Mom. You loved her and you would never let anything happen to her. We miss you and want you to come home. Shirley and grandpa and grandma are real nice and even Abby, but Dad, they are not you. We are scared sometimes that someone at night will come and take us away.

Dad we need you to protect us. We hurt so much we want you home.

Please, please, please, come home. We miss Mom and you so much. We pray you get a new trial. Anything we can do, just ask.

Love, Sara and Jake<br>
XXX XXXOXXX

# References

Heather B. Armstrong, T*he Valedictorian of Being Dead*: The True Story of Dying Ten Times to Live, New York: Gallery Books, 2019.

Isabel Wilkerson, *Caste: The Original Sin of Our Discontents*, New York: Penguin Random House, 2020.


The articles mentioned in the story are real articles that were written by me, Ron Iannone. In the story, they have been attributed to the fictionalized character Paul Testa.

Ron Iannone, "Chaos Theory and Its Implications for Curriculum and Teaching," *Education*, Vol. 115, No. 4, Summer 1995, 541–547.

Ron Iannone, "An Educator in Exile," *Journal of Instructional Psychology*, Vol. 28, No. 1, March, 2001, 38–43.

Ron Iannone, "Higher Education's Caste System," *College Student Journal*, Vol. 38, No. 1., March 2004, 9–15.

In addition, I have used versions of parts of my previously published short stories "The Private School Murder" and "Skaneateles." Those stories originally appeared in:

Ron Iannone, *Consequences: Stories, Poems, Essays*,
    Destination Press, 2015.

# Acknowledgments

I find writing to be a very lonely job. Sometimes when I struggle and end up writing a great sentence I wish there were people around to applaud. Of course when I blow it and write a god-awful sentence I expect to be booed. Anyway, I'm very lucky to have several family members and friends who are very supportive. Here are a few:

Mary, Pat, Jeff, Amita, Sonny, Joey, Mary Beth, Carl, Megan, Justin, Erin, Mason, Lisa, Adam, Bob, Christiana, Vince, Cathy, Anthony, Dot, Neil, Tom, Ken, Sharon, Steve, Michael, Bill, Susan, and several others.

I also want to thank the individuals who talked to me about their depression. Much of what they talked about was backed up by the research I found in medical journals. Moreover, I will be forever grateful to Heather Armstrong, and her book, *The Valedictorian of Being Dead*. Her thoughts about the excessive need that depressed people have for rigid schedules was very helpful. Besides this, her thoughts about huge swings of moods in depressed people were most invaluable.

Lastly, I want to thank Rae Jean and Andrew at Populore Publishing for their superb professional expertise.

# About the Author

Ron Iannone has written several books including novels, poetry, plays, essays, and works on education. He also has a love and passion for theatre and film, and he is the founder of West Virginia Public Theatre and Destination Producing. Over the course of thirty years, he has produced more than 200 theatrical productions. One screenplay he's worked on, *The Comeback*, is being considered for a film production for 2022.

Ron is professor emeritus in the College of Education and Human Services at West Virginia University. He lives with his wife in Morgantown, West Virginia; off and on they also live in Central New York. They have three adult children.